I0728414

ISBN: 978-1-9192923-9-7
Published by Late Night Books, 2025
London, United Kingdom

This is a work of fiction. The character of David Bowie appears in a fictionalised context. While inspired by the real-life individual, this portrayal is imaginative and does not claim to represent the actual person. No endorsement or involvement by the estate of David Bowie is implied. All other characters and events are fictitious; any resemblance to actual persons, living or dead, is purely coincidental.

Lyrics referenced in this work are original compositions written in homage to the spirit and tone of well-known songs. They are not reproductions of the original lyrics, but fictional reinterpretations intended as literary tribute.

Lyrics from "Wrap Your Troubles in Dreams" (1931) by Barris, Koehler & Moll appear by way of tribute. Copyright remains with the original rights holders.

Cover artwork by the author.

Second edition, November 2025

# Eden

Hadley Coull

```
EDEBIOS © 2063-2070 EDEN CORPORATION LTD.
sysbcot.exe
Initialising…
Title: Eden
Author: Hadley Coull
System.dedicated_to: Charlotte
Running diagnostics… [OK]
System: Secure
EDEN_READY
573Kb OK
END SYSBOOT_
```

For Charlotte, of course.

It is such an honour to be your father.

Sorrow hews the song, love sings it.

# Contents

DIGITAL

# London, 2063

# 1

# The Harlequin in Blue

She awoke with the sun.

Light bled through pink curtains, dappling the floor beside her. Ted-E watched as Sarah clambered out of bed.

A gasp escaped as she caught her reflection in the mirror. She wore a sequined blue dress, velvet gloves, and a silver crown. Fairy dust shimmered around her.

She tilted her head to check her hair – neatly plaited, as if by magic. Her blue shoes sparkled like diamonds. Hot air balloons drifted in and out of clouds on the wall behind her.

She burst into her parents' bedroom. 'Daddy, look. Who am I?'

She pulled the duvet back, revealing her father: broad-shouldered, unshaven, features gentled by warmth.

'*Principessa!*' Max rubbed his eyes, still half-asleep.

She squealed, 'Yay!'

'What day is it today?' he asked, feigning ignorance.

She sang brightly, 'My birthday!'

'Happy birthday, poppet!' They embraced, his stubble tickling her cheek. 'So, if you're a princess, I'm a…?'

'You're… a tiger. No—a bear. No, no—a—a tiger.'

'Good choice! Dave, can you turn me into a tiger?'

David Bowie appeared at the doorway, rendered as his *Scary Monsters* harlequin. Tangled red hair framed a frost-blue costume adorned with petals: a fragile palette of fire and ice. The costume hung off the shoulder; papery, almost flaking off his body like fading blossom.

Eyeliner and red lipstick softened his jawline. Anisocoria left one pupil dilated, so that one eye appeared brown, the other blue.

He was fragility, asymmetry, and melancholy, wrapped in petals and porcelain. The ashen fool at the end of the world. His fey beauty gave the sense that he was not of this world, but was instead a ghostly patchwork of clowns, mimes, and jesters from days gone by.

'Certainly, Max,' said Dave.

Max morphed into a more feline form. His ears pricked, whiskers sprouted, fur grew around his collar, and his nose blackened. He pulled back the duvet to reveal his furry, striped body, rendered black, white, and orange.

Sarah giggled. He really looked the part.

Max roared, 'How do I look?'

She jumped up and down on the bed. 'Yay! But where is your tail?'

He rummaged under the duvet. 'It's right here!'

***

The years had been kind to Mia. She grew more beautiful with age – becoming, not fading – and her skin spoke of a life well lived.

She sat at the dressing table in the spare room in a light gown, observing her default self – blue-eyed, brunette, poised – and wondering what to wear. She was beautiful in the classical sense that, had her life taken a different turn, she could have been a model or a film star.

The room was rendered in pastels and creams; a vintage, pastoral theme.

'Morning!' Cindy Pops appeared at the doorway.

'Hey, Cindy.'

Cindy wore her *Lustral* skin from her '48 album, *Capital Chaos*: a white, flared jumpsuit, long blond hair with purple highlights, and dewy makeup. An electric, space-age look. Max thought she was an airhead, but Mia never cared much for Bowie, either.

Mia examined herself in the mirror, wondering what to mod. 'What do you think?'

Cindy's honeyed voice soothed her. 'Your little munchkin turns five today. This calls for something special.'

'Agreed. Show me what you've got.'

'Well… We've just added the latest Max Dangerfield collection out of New York.'

A screen materialised next to the dressing table. Exquisitely dressed models appeared in a 5×4 grid, lolling and posing in pre-baked animation loops. Mia tapped on one of the models and watched her reflection fizz and glitch. White noise and a rushing sound signalled the transition, and her appearance updated accordingly.

A shimmering purple suit. Blond ponytails with braids, and wisps trailing on either side. Her makeup was bold, clean, confident.

She winced. 'Bit high society, don't you think?'

'Yeah, not quite you. How about…' – Cindy stood behind Mia and swiped left – 'smoke and silk?' Grey leather trousers, with a white cashmere jumper, matte makeup, and brown pixie hair. A bare, minimalist feel.

Mia tilted her head to one side. 'Too cold.'

'Something a bit more colourful? Check out the new geisha, 1.8. They updated the kimono.'

The graphics fizzed and Mia flickered into the skin. *Oshiroi* makeup rendered her skin ivory white and her lips scarlet red. The skin adjusted her physiognomy, rounding her face and thinning her eyebrows. She wore an artful black silk *yukata* kimono, featuring white cranes and cherry blossom trees. Her hair turned black and folded itself into *taka shimada*: a long, loose style with a high bun.

Cindy placed a hairpin through the bun to complete the look, then crouched beside Mia to finesse her makeup.

Mia ignored the construct, raising her left hand to further explore the skin. 'Nails.'

A short burst of static, and a Japanese pastoral scene rendered across her fingernails. Mist weaved in and out of pagodas. Cranes cawed as they flew across the landscape – a symbol of prosperity and good fortune. On her ring finger, Mount Fuji pierced pink skies; snow-capped and majestic. In the distance, a *shamisen* played folk music as trees rustled in the breeze.

She watched the birds glide across her nails, transfixed. 'Extend.' The nails grew a few millimetres, expanding the vista. 'More.'

Cindy finished touching up her makeup. 'You're hitting the edges of the simulation. I can't extend them any further. Too great a discrepancy between reality and the simulation will result in—'

'—visual glitches and other errors,' Mia sighed, relaxing her hand. 'Fine.' She made a good geisha – but the skin felt too elaborate for Sarah's birthday. Maybe later; a summer picnic, perhaps.

She swiped left once more. A bohemian look: a yellow summer dress, with a green floral print by Ulrika Solskjær.

'Plain Jane,' she sighed, now restless. 'Fuck it. Reset.'

She flicked through more presets.

'Hair Seven. Blond. Complexion Clear.' Always Complexion Clear.

'Lipstick. Violet.' She pouted and turned her head.

'Cheekbone width: plus five. Eyeshadow Four. Blue.' A pause. 'Lighter.'

'Sugar Plum Three.' Pink blond candy floss hair, with curls, wisps, and trails. Not quite.

'Brown Two. High Pony Three.' Nearly there.

'Body art.' She scrolled through the catalogue.

'That one. Floral Twelve, left and right. Chest Seven.'

Floral patterns etched themselves across her body, as though an invisible hand were drawing them in real time. They were coloured in the gentle, washed-out palette of old tattoos. Acacia grew on one side of her neck, blossoming beneath her ear. Ambrosia and amaryllis appeared on her chest, and a begonia flowered across her left shoulder. Flax and lilies extended the length of her arms in white and blue, tapering off on the backs of her hands.

The flowers swayed, as though caressed by a breeze. Some flowered in real time, while others would bloom at random times throughout the day.

'Nice.' Mia stood up, ready to join the others. 'Shoes Eight. Scarlet.' Suede sandals, with a thick heel.

She checked herself in the mirror and made her way downstairs.

***

Max lay in bed, tweaking settings across floating screens.

Thirty years in Eden had earned him luxuries his meagre income could never buy: a Bowie AI at his beck and call, a Jeeves bot to keep the house upright, and a bathtub carved from petrified wood, its ancient grain shot through with jasper, blue chalcedony, and opal.

'Let's see… Bowls,' he murmured. The carousel spun: stone, Moroccan, oak, mahogany, rosewood, Denby, art deco, Scandi, topaz, and ruby.

All of these could be summoned with a whisper. One only had to utter the word, and the décor would transform, flickering through static and white noise, into a new texture.

'Okay, themes…' He tapped a sequence, and the house flickered into a medieval castle, with the acoustics modified accordingly. Bare stone and woven rugs adorned each room, lit by torches and candlelight. Banners bearing the Fisher family crest graced the walls.

In the kitchen, a troupe of woodland creatures played ceremonial music as they marched across a wall: rabbits, deer, foxes, and rodents, rendered in the style of a medieval tapestry. Behind the band, a princess sang a gentle ballad, carried by servants on a litter.

Mia stood at the counter, slicing vegetables. Sarah ate quietly at the table.

'Room for a tiger?'

Mia offered a thin smile.

He slipped an arm around her waist, leaning in for a kiss. She stiffened, eased herself free, and let the peel fall into the bin.

He lowered his voice so Sarah wouldn't hear. 'Come on. It's her birthday.'

She looked him up and down. 'Are you going to stay like that all day?'

'I don't see why not. Tigers are fine creatures.'

She sighed and turned again to the chopping board.

Max sat opposite Sarah at the table. 'Jeeves, can I get some cereal please, and coffee?'

Jeeves placed a bowl of grapes on the table. 'Certainly, sir. And might I say, congratulations, Ms Fisher. Today you have reached level five!'

The service bot was cheap and mass-produced. His grey graphene-polymer exoskin stretched taut over an alloy shell. Jeeves was no visual marvel like Dave or Cindy – but he was real. He could cook, clean, vacuum, and perform other menial tasks. Though humanoid, he looked more like a puppet than a man: rubbery, awkward, and faintly grotesque.

Friends and Jeeves bots worked well together. No one wanted one without the other. Jeeves bots cleaned the house, while Friends rendered and re-skinned it in a thousand styles and colours. It was Friends who captured people's hearts and minds, but without Jeeves bots, the shelves would gather dust and the paint beneath the simulation would slowly crack and peel away.

***

A riot of colour and noise erupted in the house as the children arrived, dressed as wizards, vampires, princesses, and witches. Jeeves served the adults wine, while Dave entertained the children.

Serge and Jane – or, John and Trish – arrived, dressed immaculately. They'd met at a house party in Notting Hill four years ago, skinned as Serge Gainsbourg and Jane Birkin – late twentieth singers, style icons, and lovers – and had role-played the characters ever since.

Serge embraced Max, warm and laced with cologne. His audio plugins emulated Gainsbourg's thick, smoky drawl.

'Un tigre, hein? Magnifique. C'est sauvage.'

He glanced toward the bookcase and turntable, where a ballata record played – simple, folksy music that evoked the world of trobairitz and troubadours.

'Still hoarding antiques, mon frère?' Serge scoffed.

'For my sins,' Max replied.

Serge chuckled. 'And the bookstore? You still preaching at the temple?'

Max nodded. 'Keeping the faith.'

Serge spread his arms theatrically. 'Alors… where is the birthday girl?'

He found her eating grapes at the kitchen table, and greeted her with a kiss. 'Sarah, ma chérie. Happy birthday! How are you?'

Sarah smiled, and returned to her grapes.

Jane and Mia were chatting in the living room when Mia spotted the ring. She squealed and hugged Jane, breathless. 'Oh God! No!'

Jane blushed, eyes wide. 'It won't be until next year, but we're… well, delighted!'

The adults cheered while the children returned to their play. Serge and Jane were getting married.

Something twisted inside Max. He remembered the night they met – dancing arm in arm on a makeshift stage to a rare version of Gainsbourg's *Goodbye Emmanuelle*. They shared the vocal parts under blue and pink spotlights and love took root.

Now, four years on, they stood arm in arm once more, their love mediated through the simulation. Had they ever seen each other's true forms? Did they disable their skins behind closed doors? Did they even remember who they were beneath their masks? Was the relationship built on genuine connection and intimacy, or merely the fantasy of living someone else's life?

Dave led the children outside – the harlequin in blue, the Pied Piper from outer space, masked in grief, ribboned in wit.

As Sarah stepped into the garden, soldiers atop ramparts blew horns, beginning the festivities.

'All hail, Princess Sarah!' they announced, then sounded a fanfare. Banners unfurled down the house's walls, each bearing hand-drawn pictures of Sarah.

The children sat amid blankets and cushions. A unicorn grazed at the back of the garden, fairy dust sparkling in the air around it. The children stared at Dave as they settled, wondering who this strange, funny man was – and indeed, whether he ever was a man.

Mia crossed the garden and stepped into a zone she'd pre-set to suppress noise and effects – a sanctuary for the adults.

She sat with friends while Max knelt with the children.

Jane sat next to Mia, who poured tea. Jane leaned in, laughing, 'I see Max is enjoying himself.'

Though she longed to sink into a hole, Mia only winced. 'Yes. I expect so.'

Across the garden, Max shushed the crowd and signalled. 'Shhh, guys. Dave's gonna start the show!'

He began with mime, working through the classics: trapped in a box, eating a banana, moonwalk.

Then, with a wink, he plucked a ball from behind his ear – then another, and another, then more still – until he was juggling nine, the air flickering with tumbling colour.

He dropped to one knee and let them fall, mouth wide – the balls vanished down his throat in one impossible gulp.

The children roared with laughter.

Mia pressed her teacup to her lips, eyes fixed on the harlequin.

The ground bloomed – balloons sprouted and drifted upwards, some shaped like animals, others like mythical beasts. The children stood, entranced, as more and more rose into the sky.

Sarah reached for a red balloon as it rose from the ground, but her hand passed through the image, breaking the illusion.

'Ah, ah,' Dave interrupted. He crouched, whispering to Sarah, 'Remember – me, the balloons – sounds and pictures. We're not really here. But there's something I need to show you,' his voice shifted, low and grave, 'and this is most definitely real.'

He stepped aside, his arms guiding Sarah towards the table behind him, where a pink birthday cake sat in the shape of a dragon. Jellies formed its scales; red liquorice, its fiery breath.

Dave stepped back as the children descended upon the cake.

As the guests gathered, Dave clicked his fingers. An old upright piano sprouted from the garden fence, trundling along on its wheels until parked flush against the fence from which it had emerged.

He sat down, strummed the keys from high to low, then addressed the crowd as Max lit candles. 'Ladies and gentlemen, please join me in song to celebrate the most wonderful,' – a C chord – 'charming,' – a G7 – 'lady what I have ever known,' – an F chord.

The guests joined in as Dave sang.

*Happy birthday to you,*
*Happy birthday to you,*
*Happy birthday, dear Sarah,*
*Happy birthday to you.*

As the applause faded, Sarah pointed to the sky. 'Look.' she cried. All eyes followed her gaze.

Thousands of balloons drifted overhead, swirling around dragons adorned with gems and jewellery. The creatures flapped their wings, shaping the balloons into a shimmering rainbow. Gasps and coos rippled through the crowd.

Max called to Sarah, 'Sarah, the candles! Come on: make a wish!'

She blew out the candles, barely extinguishing all five, then wrapped her arms around her father. Above them, the rainbow burst, glitter spilling across the city below.

***

She stood in front of the mirror, let out a sigh, and swiped left. Her dress and fairy wings dissolved in a shimmer of light and dust.

She brushed her teeth, then called Max upstairs, her mind fizzing.

'Daddy, where does Dave sleep?'

'He doesn't,' Max said, tucking her in. 'He just freezes, like a statue, and stays like that. It's like turning a machine off. Look, I'll show you.'

He called to the house. 'Dave, sleep mode.'

Dave entered and stood in the centre of the room. 'Certainly.'

A fizz of white noise and static, and he rendered as his *Heroes* album cover: a black and white statue staring into empty space. He held one hand upright – angular, jagged – the other against his chest. A gentle blue mist rose from his body, signalling his stasis.

Sarah grimaced, 'I don't like it.'

'No problem.' Max clicked his fingers. 'Wake up.'

Dave transformed into the harlequin amid crackle and white noise, then stepped aside, awaiting further instructions.

'Daddy, I want to be a princess tomorrow.'

'Yeah, but it's just for birthdays for now, poppet. You shouldn't spend too much time in Eden.'

'Why?'

'So that you know what's real and what's not real.'

'Why?'

'Well, because the real world is all we really have.'

A pause. 'But is Rapunzel real?'

'She's not real, but she is *true*.'

Sarah looked at him blankly.

'It's the kind of truth you feel, not touch. A good story lets us feel something real.'

Sarah nodded. 'But you had Eden when you were five. I want the dragons to live here.'

'Eden was simpler back then. Not so… impressive. More like a picture book. Now it's… almost too real.'

'Hmmm,' she murmured, unconvinced.

'See, it's harder for children to understand what's real and what's not real - so most of the time it's just for adults.'

She looked down and played with her fingers.

'Hey, I know. It's not easy being five, is it?'

He pressed his forehead to Sarah's, raised his right hand. They shook pinkies. 'Hey, don't worry. You'll be alright. Pinkie promise.'

He readied himself to leave. 'Come on, monkey. It's nearly ten. Bedtime.' He clasped his hands together, and pretended to sleep. 'Come on, zzzzzz. Sweet dreams, love.'

'Sweet dreams I love you.'

He kissed her forehead and whispered goodnight.

Though tired, she lay awake for a while listening to her parents argue.

***

'They were laughing at me, Max. Laughing at me,' Mia snapped across the kitchen table.

A render of De Chirico's *Mystery and Melancholy of a Street* hung on the wall – backlit, given depth, as though it breathed light.

'What's the problem? Nobody cried. Nobody died. Sarah had fun. Isn't that enough?'

'Max, it's not real. All these… bloody illusions. It's too much. I don't want it for my daughter.'

Max toyed with the edge of the table, then lifted his eyes to hers. '*Your* daughter?'

'It's not good to live in these dream worlds, Max. And how much did this even cost?'

'It comes with the sub. You mean *our* daughter, right?'

The air thickened. A silence they both knew too well.

'Not now, Max.' She rose, carrying her teacup to the sink.

'What do you mean, *your* daughter?' His voice followed her across the kitchen.

She set the cup down hard, porcelain on marble. 'I need to think of Sarah, that's all.'

'You mean *we* need to think of Sarah.'

'Oh, forget it.' Her back was still to him. 'I'm tired, Max. Why do we always end up here?'

'Because you always bring us here,' he said, softer than he meant to.

She stared at the floor as though it might yield an answer. Then half-sang, almost to herself, 'Round and round the merry-go-round… Max, we've had this conversation a hundred times—'

'—But nothing ever gets said.'

With a clink she set the teapot down, her hands trembling just enough to betray her. 'I'm not doing this again. Not now.'

'We already are.'

She shook her head. 'I don't… I don't know what you want from me any more.'

'I want to know what happened to you.'

Somehow, somewhere along the way, they had become strangers again, as on the day they had met.

She sighed, walking away. 'Goodnight, Max.'

'Where did I go wrong, Mia?' His voice cracked as it chased her down the hallway. 'Where did I go wrong?'

He sat in the silence she left behind.

Sarah and Mia: the elixir and the vampire. One gave life; the other drained it. The child hallowed as the lover hollowed.

For one he poured love, for the other, he forged armour.

The space between them, once filled with love, now knew only ache. In time, he made his way to bed, lying far from the warmth of her body.

***

One night, a few weeks later, a storm raged across the city. As London slept, a lightning bolt struck near the Fisher house – bright red, with a black and blue outline.

The next morning, Max awoke to an empty bed and a quiet house. He found a note on the kitchen table.

> *Max.*
> *I can't go on like this. I need to get away for a while.*
> *Take care of Sarah.*
> *Mia*

He crumpled the paper lightly, checking it was real and not one of Dave's pranks. He looked around, half-expecting Dave or Mia to leap out, laughing at him.

The ink smudged.

He heard Sarah stir. His heart raced, wondering what he would say to her.

Over eggs and soldiers, she asked, 'Where is Mummy?'

'Her friend's sick, so Mummy's gone to look after her. But don't worry, love. She's not gone far, and she'll be back soon.'

'How many days?'

'I don't know. Maybe three or four. Let's see. She's gonna call later. We can ask her then, okay?'

Sarah looked towards the garden, deep in thought. Mia had never left her like this before.

She picked up a finger puppet from the table, slipped it on, and made it dance, singing faintly, 'Let's make a tea party… but where is Ted-E?'

'Yeah, let's have a tea party. But first, love, look at me.' He took her hands in his. 'It's okay, alright? Mummy's just a bit sad and she needs to see her friend. But don't worry. She'll be back soon.'

But Mia didn't come back. Max and Sarah were on their own.

# London, 2070

# 2

# Patch Notes

'No, on the side. She likes berries on the side.'

Max worked the pans while the droid arranged the garnish. Pancakes.

'Yes, sir.'

'Hey.' Sarah appeared at the doorway, buttoning her cardigan. Blond hair brushed her shoulders and her blue eyes caught the morning light.

'Hey, love. Look,' Max gestured towards the pans, 'your favourite.'

'I'm fine. I'll eat at school.' She adjusted her clothes, readying herself to leave.

Max hesitated. 'Hey – can I grab you for a sec? Quick word about Saturday.'

He sat at the table, nudging a chair out with his foot – a quiet invitation.

'Daddy, I need to go. I'm gonna be late.'

'Two minutes, okay? I need to ask about your birthday. I thought we might go to Little Venice. Remember? The boats? The hot chocolate place?'

Sarah fidgeted. 'I don't know. Mum's booked something. Spa, I think.'

'A spa? But it's my turn this year and your mum knows it.'

'I know. But… I kind of want to go.' She looked away, brushing her hair behind one ear. 'She said I could bring Jemma.'

'Jemma?' His voice caught. 'I thought it was our day.'

'I'm sorry. It's just… we did Little Venice last year. It's kind of… for kids.'

'Okay, well… Let's see, yeah?'

'Mhm.' She grabbed orange juice from the fridge and took a sip. 'Daddy, have you heard of Alternate Resistance?'

Max smirked. 'You mean Analogue Resistance?'

'Yeah, is it true that they live underground? Katie told me they live in the sewers and they eat rats.'

Max laughed, 'I think she's just trying to scare you. They're a strange sort, but I don't think they eat rats. All they do is cause trouble and drive up sub prices.'

She put the juice back in the fridge. 'Okay. I need to go.'

'Okay, okay. Off you go.'

He called after her as she walked away. 'Hey! No hug for your old man?'

She offered a limp, perfunctory embrace.

'What, I have to ask for a cuddle now?'

'Daddy, I'm gonna be late.' She slipped into the hallway as Jeeves served Max a pancake he no longer felt like eating.

Perhaps he coddled her too much – smothered her, even. Or perhaps this was simply the way of things: the slow unspooling, the gentle untethering, as the girl gave way to the woman.

She paused at the mirror, humming a pop song, checking that he wasn't looking – then leaned in, double-tapping her eyelids. Blue eyeshadow bloomed. A swipe of her finger summoned matte lipstick.

'Hey!' Max watched her from the kitchen doorway. 'What did we agree? Not until you're older.'

'But why?'

'Because I don't want you wearing this yet.'

'But you said that last year.'

'Yeah, and it's still true.'

'But it de-renders at the school gates. I told you.'

He held her gaze just long enough to make her squirm.

She huffed and swiped her reflection, wiping the effects away.

'And autotune. Off.'

'But Daddy, my spots. They'll eat me alive if I—'

'—Sarah. Turn it off.'

'But you can't, and anyway, why do you get to decide? It's my face.' Her voice cracked – not defiant, but raw.

He stepped in gently. 'Hey, what is it? What's up?'

She tried to shake her head but her body betrayed her. Her lip trembled.

'*Default.* They call me default,' she mumbled.

'Why? What for?'

'I'm basic – no skins, no nothing, because you don't let me.'

Tears broke free and traced a line down her cheek. Max caught them with the back of his hand. 'Sweetheart… Look at you. You have the most beautiful skin. You don't need any of this.'

She said nothing.

'Come on. They're just kids. They don't know any better.'

She sniffed, staring at the floor.

'Hey, I'm glad you told me, okay? That took guts. And look, in a year or two, you'll be able to do all the makeup and filters you like. Just… not yet, love.'

She sniffed, and drew a breath. 'Yeah, well – it won't matter, 'cause you can't afford it anyway.'

She turned and left. 'Don't call me at school.'

Max sighed, leaned against the wall, and noticed Jeeves at the kitchen door, quietly watching the humans argue.

The droid offered a clumsy imitation of Max's sigh, stepped back, and returned to his duties.

***

The art of femto-photography, or *light in flight*, had recently been patched in. The technique recorded video at such high speeds that it could reveal the very movement of light through three-dimensional space. Software slowed the footage so that humans could watch light fill a room as its wavefront rippled through the space.

Through femto, light took its time, modulating the physics of illumination to make space for tenderness. Femto framed light as a lover – delicate, lingering, sensorial – intimacy slowed to the speed of longing.

Traditionally, turning on a light resulted in the immediate illumination of a room. With femto patched in, home lighting became a sublime experience – something approaching an art form.

Light became sculpture. Time became texture.

Artists and sculptors embraced femto to create intoxicating works: spectral traces, lingering light bubbles, and sculptures made of light forms and wavelengths which had no equivalence in the physical world.

So it was that when Max entered the bathroom that evening, the light did not fill the room instantly or linearly; but rather, slowly, organically, and messily. Like water in space, the light pooled and swirled, painting the room in colour.

A cool turquoise lit the floor. As it rose, it bled into magenta, birthing red-orange filaments that crawled up the walls like flames. The colours danced with each other, intermixed, and formed new hues.

Azure spotlights lit the bathwater from below the waterline. Candles with pink flames self-lit around the rim of the bathtub. Steam rose from the water, warming the room.

At one end of the bath, a gramophone no bigger than a cupcake spun a tiny record. Max's sessions with Dr Anderson always began with Tchaikovsky's *Arabian Dance*, a soothing piece that evoked the mystery of faraway lands. Holographic ballet dancers, a few inches tall, hovered above the gramophone; translucent and ghostly. Their edges crackled and fizzed as they mixed with the coloured light around them.

Dr Anderson was a red-eyed tree frog; bright green, and with yellow and blue stripes down his side. His sticky webbed feet shone orange beneath two bulbous red eyes. He was a squat little creature, who spent his days philosophising and eating grubs.

Max spotted the doctor lying beneath the bonsai tree at one end of the bath. 'Hey, doc.'

The doctor spoke in a solemn, refined British voice. 'Hello, Max. Has it been a week already?' He stretched and clambered down to a lily pad which floated in the bath. 'I suppose it has. How quickly the days go by…

'And where shall we travel to this evening?' The frog knew the answer, but he asked anyway.

'Rainforest.' As Max lowered himself into the bath, the bathroom walls folded outwards and fell away, revealing an expansive night-time scene. Only the bath, floor, and door remained intact – now perched on a platform above a jungle canopy that stretched to the horizon. The air hummed with the sounds of cicadas and birdsong. Rustling and scowls below, as critters foraged in the undergrowth.

He looked upward as the night unfolded. 'Let there be stars, let there be night, and let there be light.'

The Milky Way arced across the sky, revealing a hundred billion stars. Comets fell from the west, their tails streaking across the night sky. To the north, the aurora borealis, where ghostly towers of green, pink, and purple shimmered in the solar wind. The moon loomed large in the east at 5× magnification.

'A full moon tonight.' Dr Anderson observed.

'Madness approaches.'

'Perhaps.' A housefly buzzed around the frog. As it passed before him, Dr Anderson's tongue shot out at lightning speed. The fly was devoured, and that was the end of his story.

'Moon's too bright,' said Max, squinting. He raised his hand and pinched the moon between his thumb and forefinger, shrinking it back to its default size. Max leaned back, exhaled, and let his body sink into the water.

'How are you, Max?' asked the frog.

'I'm better now,' he said, letting his body relax, rolling his head from side to side.

'And how have you been?'

A pause. Max stirred the water with one hand. 'She's pulling away again. Doesn't want to hang out.' He exhaled softly, watching ripples drift outward. 'I keep trying to mend what broke. I just… don't know if I'm getting through.'

He gave a small shake of the head. 'I miss her. I miss when she let me in.'

He took a sip of the whisky he'd brought. 'You give them the best years of your life. Teach them, hold them, pour everything you've got into them. First they need you, then they love you, then they see through you, then they leave… and if you're lucky, years later, they might just forgive you.'

He shrugged. 'Maybe that's fine. Maybe I just suck it up. I guess we'll always have the memories.'

'They come back, Max,' said the frog, softly. 'They come back.'

'I still feel it. The guilt.'

'The breakup.'

Max nodded.

'It's been seven years, Max.' The frog inched closer – a gesture of compassion. 'Yet Mia still haunts you.'

'The elixir and the vampire. One gives life; the other takes it away.'

'Mia is long gone—'

'—yet her spirit lingers.'

'Indeed.' The frog tilted his head upward, as if gesturing to the house. 'She lives here, with us – a ghost, animated by guilt.'

'Can you taste it in the air, doc? It's eating away at me.'

'Mia made her choices. She abandoned Sarah. If I may be so bold, she is lucky to even see her. You were the victim, Max, not her.'

Max passed a hand across his face, his voice hollow.

'How do I learn to live with it, doc? The pain, it won't go away.'

He looked up, voice cracking slightly.

'Tell me it's going to be okay, doc. You said it'd be okay.'

The frog let the silence breathe for a moment.

'I didn't say it would be okay. I said I would be here with you.' He adjusted his stance, sending a ripple across the bathwater. 'Sometimes wounds don't heal, Max – yet we learn to live with them.'

A pause.

Max looked away, his voice barely audible. 'What do we do when the dreams die, doc?'

'We dream anew,' the frog replied. 'And that is why we are here: not to erase your pain, but to walk beside it.'

'Feels like she's taking out her pain on me.'

'Adolescence is a strange and… *unique* experience. Her body is changing, as is her mind. She's growing up, that's all.'

'Right? Soon I won't even *be* her Daddy. I'll be her Dad.' He looked the frog in the eye. 'She'll make her own way in the world.'

'And where will that leave you?'

'Sitting in my bath, talking to a tree frog?' He sighed and swung his feet onto the bath's rim, toes dripping.

The frog hopped onto another lily pad to be closer to Max. 'We are never alone, Max. To love one's child is to let them go,' his voice softened, 'when the time comes.'

'I guess so.' Max gazed into the distance as his hands played with the bathwater.

'Be her safe space. Encourage her autonomy. Trust that if she pulls away, it means you've done something right,' the frog said, though he could see that Max was no longer listening. The session, it seemed, was over.

After a pause, he concluded, 'Well, that's it for another week. Go well, Max.' Dr Anderson climbed up the side of the bath, nestled under the bonsai tree, and slept.

'So long, Doc.'

A single cherry blossom petal, loosened from the bonsai, drifted onto the bathwater and began to spin in slow, widening circles.

He raised his head and spoke to the room.

'Dating. TV.'

A portrait screen materialised to his left, showing videos of single women. To his right, a smaller landscape screen appeared, playing the news at a whisper. The screens displayed volumetric video – spatial, holographic imagery captured by hundreds of drones in a spherical formation. The resultant video appeared not as a flat image on a 2D plane, but as a three-dimensional space that faded at the edges.

He leaned back and relaxed.

A gym bunny, lithe, energised and effusive. 'Hey, guys! I'm a fun-loving girl, looking for someone who doesn't take themselves too serious—'

'—No.' Her video faded away to the left.

A morose, gothic figure, partly obscured by shadow. 'No ONS, no deviant creeps, no—'

'—No, no, no, no.'

A homely, motherly type, in a rustic setting. 'Let's cry, laugh, learn, grow, and love togeth—'

'—No! Christ, who says this kind of thing?' The carousel spun on.

An artistic, unpretentious type. 'Know that you will be obliged to listen to me play my recorder every Christmas, and you also need to pretend to like my cooking—'

'—Hello, Eva. Like.'

A generic female voice responded. 'Would you like to leave a message?'

'No.' Max's voice trailed off as his eyes drifted to the smaller screen, which showed burning buildings. He flicked the dating screen away to watch the news.

A female voice narrated, '…here in Euston presents a tremendous challenge to firefighters. It seems the terrorists were targeting a local node to reduce citywide bandwidth. We believe they failed, but we're awaiting confirmation from Eden.'

Max muttered, 'Tossers, pushing up sub prices. Go back to the forest if you don't like it here.'

Then, to the room, 'Light news.'

The feed switched to the ISS Orbital, suspended two hundred and fifty miles above Earth. A gold-plated probe was docking in the station's construction bay. Women in orange spacesuits drifted around it; in the foreground, a woman in white addressed the camera.

Max pinched the screen, enlarging it.

A perky voice chimed in. 'Yes Mike, and it's great to be here on the ISS Orbital, where – as we can see – the Omac fusion core is being fitted to the *Odysseus* probe. One year from today, humanity will launch its first interstellar mission to Alpha Centauri – our next-door neighbour in the cosmos!'

As Max soaped his arms and neck, the broadcast continued.

'In 2068, China's FAST telescope picked up radio signals from Proxima b, resembling early-twentieth media and denoting the presence of intelligent lifeforms. The source: a potentially Earth-like planet called Proxima b in the Centauri system.

'Backed by Eden CEO Vegas Delaney, the *Odysseus* probe is a £900 billion joint project between ServTec and Apex Industries. Here's Delaney speaking earlier.'

The video cut to Britain's most famous man. Vegas Delaney – billionaire, visionary, aesthete – stood at a podium, flashing square glasses, long black hair, and a silver goatee.

The camera lingered as a voiceover filled in the gaps. He'd made early breakthroughs in optical tech – including the EYEsight lens, which rendered traditional screens obsolete overnight, and changed the cultural life of the West forever.

Then came personal tragedy: the ocean took his wife and child in a storm. He buried his grief in code, building Virtua Systems – later Eden – a virtual double of the physical world.

Eden 1.0 launched in 2042, a sanctuary for a collapsing civilisation. The platform absorbed all media into one immersive world, and gave rise to new forms of expression previously unimaginable. Life became more exhilarating with each day that passed. By the mid-fifties, many could barely remember life before Eden, and most didn't want to, either.

Walls of cameras whirred and flashed as Delaney leaned into the mic.

'It fills me with such pride and joy to install the Omac core. One year from now, God willing, we will depart these humble shores, and begin our ascent towards the stars.

'Who knows what wonders this probe shall reveal, and our descendants shall witness?'

Max got out and dried himself.

The video cut back to the reporter. 'Travelling at 99.9896% the speed of light, *Odysseus* will arrive in January 2076 – with a message of peace from Earth. And who knows? One day we might even meet them in person! This is Lauren Jay, BBC News, reporting from the ISS Orbital 3.4.'

'Pause.' The video froze on a wide shot of the station. A slender cylinder extended nearly a mile into the distance; parasol at one end, observatory at the other. Max angled his head to explore the far side. He raised his hand and let it pass through the golden probe. A low hum rose as his hand intercepted the screen, and he dreamed of life beyond our star system.

'Dinner is ready, sir,' said Jeeves, from the doorway.

Max blinked, surfacing from the dream. 'On my way.'

The rainforest melted away as he stepped from the room, revealing the bathroom, sparsely decorated and perfunctory.

Jeeves added the finishing touches to dinner. A Chezz™ board lay on the dining table, creatures scattered across its 8×8 grid. A campfire burned on D6, tended by a bard on C7. The bard, Tiki, suffered from insomnia and sat up most nights playing ballads on her lute.

Max held his palm above the board and swept it aside to make space. The creatures stirred and grumbled as they were woken.

'Sorry, sorry. Go back to sleep.' They settled again as Max turned to Jeeves. 'Alright, what have we got?'

'Risotto, sir.'

'Again?'

'I'm sorry, sir. I couldn't get anything fresh in. It's a pumpkin risotto, sir, with a dash of lemon.' Jeeves poured wine. 'Bon appétit, sir, and if I may, sir, I will attend to the bathroom.'

As Max ate, a pulsating red circle appeared in the top right of his field of vision. A notification.

'What is it?'

His utility software appeared. Devi, Great Goddess, Mahadevi, Divine Mother, Lakshmi, Kali, Durga, Jaganmata, Mother of the Universe glided into the kitchen, sitting cross-legged on a floating cashmere carpet. She was beautiful, radiant; her poise channelling the grace of the seven heavens. Her *makuta* crown sparkled with emeralds, amethyst, and peridot. She held a trident, a sword, and a bowl of rice in three of her hands, leaving the fourth free. Her tiger, Somanandin, lay by her side, watching Max and flicking its tail.

'Namaste.' She brought her palms together and bowed her head as she approached. Devi rendered at half scale – about three feet tall – and spoke in the soft, melodic cadence of southern India.

'I trust you are well?'

'Hey. What's up, Devi?'

'Sir, the new patch is ready for installation.'

He sighed. 'Another patch?' He looked away. 'And every time we pretend we're fixed.'

'Stability remains a work in progress, sir. Repair is part of the ritual.'

'But of course it is. So… you got some good stuff?'

'Always, sir. Would you like to view the patch notes?'

He glanced at his plate. Plenty of time. 'Sure.'

A screen appeared, showing Delaney's introduction. He leaned against a desk in his executive suite, London's cityscape in the background. 'Welcome to a world where dreams come true. Welcome—'

'—Can we skip this? I must have seen this bit fifty —'

'—It will just be a moment, sir,' Devi said. 'I think the introduction is designed to settle the audience.'

Delaney continued, 'You know, our technology is so good, that people say it's more real than reality.' The camera cut to a close up. 'In Eden, you can be whoever you want to be, make the world in your own image. Eden. *Your world, your way.*'

The film cut to a sequence of vignettes designed to showcase the new features, as a female voice narrated.

- The seven Divines now more likely to visit users unannounced
- Improved alcohol and drug mechanics
- More bees
- New mod: *The Great Forest of London*. Bring a fresh, luscious look to London with this tasteful forest habitat, featuring over seventy types of trees, mosses, and ivies

'Wait. I like that. Install.'

'Very good, sir.'

- Update: *Electric Tweens* store rebooted! Plus, we're proud to introduce *Ikimono* nail friends – the hottest tween craze, fresh out of Japan

On-screen, cartoon animals appeared across a girl's fingernails. On one nail, a black cat scowled at the camera, then winked.

Max enthused, 'She's been going on about this for months.' He glanced towards the house and called, 'Hey, Sarah!'

AI AND FRIENDS

- Improved Jeeves' cooking skills. No longer burns toast
- New Utility skins, including Devi, Shiva, medic, and Archangel

Max turned to Devi. 'You got a new skin? Preview.'

Devi spun in a blur to transform into Saraswati, goddess of knowledge, music, the arts, wisdom, and learning. She was dressed in a white sari and held a veena guitar. Her flying carpet morphed into a white lotus, and her tiger into a blue-green hummingbird, Gutna, which hovered beside her.

She rested a hand on her waist. 'How do I look?'

'Divine. Keep it.'

She tipped her head, acknowledging the compliment, as the video continued.



Max raised an eyebrow. 'Seriously?'

'Remnant of old code that treated animals as non-playable characters. Foxes would hold a grudge against people who cleared out their bins too often. They'd poop in their front garden and howl at their houses late at night. It would go on for months. The code's been cleaned up now.'

'Er… Okay.'

He swiped the screen, which disappeared in a cloud of dust, then turned to Devi. 'We done?'

'Yes, sir. Would you like to apply the update?'

'Sure.'

Devi looked to one side and placed a finger on her temple. After a moment, she spoke. 'I'm afraid you lack the funds to purchase the new patch, sir.'

'What do you mean? There should be…' He looked at Dave, who stood leaning against the doorframe, arms folded.

Dave shook his head. 'Sorry, old chap. Bad month at the store. People just aren't reading as much as they used to.'

Max turned again to Devi. 'But I – come on, Dev, I need this. It's been a tough day.'

'I'm afraid this would breach protocol, sir. I cannot perform the upgrade.'

'Bollocks.' He gritted his teeth, racking his brain for ideas. After a moment, he crossed the kitchen and began rummaging through a drawer. 'Should have just the thing… somewhere in here.'

The intercom hung on the wall in the hallway: a hardware interface for emergencies and software failures. About the size of a briefcase, the device featured a sleek white casing, an eight-inch nanocell screen, and a foldout keyboard on the underside.

He found the dongle – a device that could access cracked versions of Eden software and upgrades. He'd won the device in a card game in Soho one night.

A sticker on the dongle read:

# CRANKY'S CRACKS

He hurried to the hallway. 'What did he say again… Plug it in and reboot?'

The device whirred and clicked as it connected to the intercom. 'Alright, this should patch things up.'

He called to Devi, 'Okay, Dev. Just rebooting. Be right back.'

'Sir, you—'

He rebooted while she was mid-sentence, freezing the construct. Gutna hung limp in the air beside her, wings outstretched.

A powering-down sound. Animations hung in stasis. The room darkened, colours draining to greyscale – the mark of suspended software.

He knew enough about code to know better.

He exhaled – then pressed the reboot button.

Much as a genie appears almost instantly when summoned from a lamp, transforming the energy of a room, so too did Cranky materialise in Max's hallway. Yet, though he carried a trace of the delirious energy of a djinn, Cranky was an altogether less impressive figure. A squat man in oil-stained overalls and a lumberjack shirt, tool belt at his waist, face crumpled by life. His skin was blotched, his clothes frayed, yet he fizzed with a nervous charge, as though patched together from broken code.

Cranky appeared at a quarter scale, hovering in the air before Max. An over-sized stopwatch hung in the air beside him, its hands ticking backwards.

'Welcome to Cranky's Cracks, for all your software needs,' he rasped. 'Hacks, exploits, regrades, reboots – all straight through the firewall. Whatever you need, I'll crank it open. Quick, though. Clock's ticking.' He tapped the stopwatch, initiating the time.

Max hesitated. 'So what do I—?'

Cranky cut across him, muttering to himself as he examined the intercom. 'Let's see… model sixty-three, version two. Old bones, but not as old as me.' He chuckled – a dry, broken sound.

From nowhere, a child's voice whispered, 'Thirty seconds remaining.'

Cranky prised open a panel to check serial numbers. 'Standard protocol, sixteen-tera flash… ah. Got your wisp wired in, too. Still breathing down here?' He tilted his head, listening for its reply.

Max frowned. 'Er, can I just get the new patch?'

Cranky looked up and smiled. 'That all? After all this? Fine.'

He inhaled sharply and dived into the machine.

'Twenty seconds remaining,' the child intoned.

Sparks hissed inside the intercom, the sound of spanners ratcheting and metal grinding.

Max glanced at the timer and wondered if, in unleashing Cranky, he'd bitten off more than he could chew. 'So, what happens at zero?'

Cranky's voice echoed from deep inside the hardware. 'Dunno. Never got that far.'

'Ten seconds remaining.'

Max wiped his palms against his trousers.

Cranky surfaced, grinning. 'All patched. Good to go.' He tapped the stopwatch, freezing it at 0:01.82, and vanished in a puff of black static.

Silence.

The room remained in greyscale. Devi and Dave hung in stasis.

'Did it work?'

Text flickered in the air before him:

```
Warning. Installation corrupted.
Three errors total.
```

A low hum emanated from the kitchen – faint at first, then louder. The greyscale light pulsed into topaz blue, as though something breathed inside the system.

As he approached, the light birthed a portal – a ragged aperture a few feet wide, its edges crackling.

Within the corrupted image, a glyph formed.

Max froze, wondering if Cranky had somehow opened a back door to his system.

Muffled voices seeped through, blurred, as though underwater. Fragments of speech broke the static.

A man's voice: '…can't get a lock… closing in.'

Then a woman: '…signal's weak… isolate…'

Shadows coalesced inside the aperture. Three, maybe four silhouettes, hunched as though gathered around a console, their faces indistinct.

Another voice cut through, strong and deliberate, female. 'To the dreambound of Eden. I speak from across the void—'

The portal flickered, fractured, then steadied.

Max's throat tightened. The words slipped out, barely audible, 'What…?'

The woman's voice persisted through the crackle, '…oppressed majority. The life you lead is not your own. Seek—'

The signal collapsed, then reasserted. '...Seek the resistance. Find the truth. Seek the resistance. Find the truth.'

The words looped, broken.

A ringing sound rose in Max's ears, drilling inward. He staggered back, clutching his skull. His fingers scrabbled for the intercom, finding the emergency controls. He flipped a red switch and punched the reboot button.

The portal imploded in an instant. Silence.

A clean, bright tone signalled the reboot. Lighting and sounds returned to their default settings.

Lines of code crawled across Max's vision in cool blue, accompanied by the faint clicks of old machines booting back to life:

```
EDEBIOS © 2063-2070 EDEN CORPORATION LTD.
AURA SYS-K 402 BIOS revision 0703
sysboot.exe
Initialising…
Eden v.2.6.1
Detecting implants… OK
Primary User (1) Max Fisher
Secondary User (2) Sarah Fisher
Intercom: v.1.7.3
Utility: Devi v.3.1.4 (Saraswati)
Friend: Bowie v.1.8.12 (Harlequin)
Wisp: Willow v.2.2.0 (Electric Blue)
Counsel: Frog v.2.3.2
Mods ENABLED
The Great Forest of London
Seaside Pastels
Initialising Mods… OK
892Tb OK
END SYSBOOT_
```

The code faded away as Devi unpaused. '—do not need to reboot your system.'

She looked away and touched her temple. 'Correction, sir. Eden 2.6.1 successfully installed.' She paused, her image distorting for a moment, then stabilising. 'Well, I wish you good evening and please let me know if I can be of further assistance.' She glided away on her lotus.

He looked around, bewildered, then saw Sarah standing at the top of the stairs. 'What's wrong?' she asked.

'Nothing. Got the new patch. It's got those nails you wanted.'

She gasped, beamed, and vanished into her room.

'Hope it was worth it.'

He stretched his jaw and leaned against the wall. 'What the *hell* was that?'

***

He crept downstairs. Dave played a haunting melody on the piano – a classical piece that Max couldn't quite place. Jeeves sat on the sofa opposite, watching Dave.

Max whispered to the bot, 'Okay, hook me up.'

'At this hour, sir? Are you sure that's—'

'—Come on, man. She's asleep, and I wanna try out the new patch. Besides,' he adopted an aloof tone, quoting an old philosopher, 'one should go out of one's mind at least once a day. It is only by going out of one's mind that one comes to one's senses.'

Unable to formulate a meaningful objection, Jeeves opened a panel in his chest and handed the neon to Max.

He sparked up in his bedroom. His spoon had corroded and thinned out. Though neon was cheap, the gold spoon burned a hole in users' pockets, and another one in their nose.

He breathed in the sweet fumes.

As the powder sparked, he fell onto the bed – drifting through colour, a dream in slow bloom.

Fractals, nebulae, ghosts of past lovers drifted past.

Beside him bobbed Boo: a rotund, pixelated, two-frame creature, somewhere between a cat, dog, and rabbit. Boo squeaked and squelched along a psychedelic path through the cosmos, gently guiding Max as he cascaded downwards.

As Max's head hit the pillow, the hallucinations softened and he grew drowsy. The colours dissipated, and he found himself in his bedroom again, crumpled on the bed, eyes twitching, half-open. Boo perched on the pillow beside him, watching over him as he fell asleep.

A blood moon shone on the wall opposite, casting a gentle nightlight. As Max passed out, snow fell all around him, and a cold wind whispered through the room.

# 3

# Nox Aeterna

A hard rain fell in Soho.

Jak skulked under the awning of a Piccadilly sex shop. Across the street, crowds poured into famed nightclub Nox Aeterna for Atrocity Engine's first UK gig.

'You saw her buy the tickets?' he barked to his wisp, Mephistopheles.

'Told you twice already. Her and her scrawny boyfriend. Saw them on Shaftesbury.' The drone hovered overhead, scanning the crowd.

'They pay cash?'

'Affirmative.'

The softpunk cowboy turned his collar up and slouched against the wall. His leather coat hung to his knees, fox fur at the collar. Chains rattled from his boots. Purple-silver hair spilled across his shoulders. A neon skull ring lit one hand; a topaz snake the other. Glyphs coiled his right arm like tattoos.

He was pure twentieth – glamour, rot, and a smile you couldn't trust.

'C'm'ere, boy.' Jak lit a cigarette as Fang prowled the street, marking and protecting his territory. The spectral white wolf appeared as a translucent, ghostly mirage. Fang joined his master under the overhang, shook the rain from his fur, and sat down.

'C'mon, c'mon, c'mon. Where the fuck is she?'

Jak drew on a cigarette glowing purple at the tip. He'd set tips to render in random colours, skewing towards purples and blues – shades that evoked the kind of inner calm which Jak often sought, yet never seemed to find.

'Relax, Jak. You're making me nervous,' the wisp replied. The spherical droid hovered at eye level, no bigger than a tennis ball. Circuitry and cabling throbbed across his black frame like human veins, sparking and pulsating seemingly at random. On his front face, a 4:3 projector screen displayed a blue human eye that blinked in real time.

Jak had given Mephistopheles a deep, synthesised voice – brooding, monotone – in homage to the old sci-fi films he'd watched as a kid.

'Fuck off, man. I'm pumped for the hit,' Jak barked.

'Relax. We'll get her. Delaney will be pleased,' the droid said.

'Yeah. Gotta keep the d-d-dreamers d – dreaming.' His voice caught, stuttering. A shader subroutine emulated a DJ scratching over breaks to mask his tic, mixing his voice with breaks and samples.

The night sky pulsed with pinks and blues. Neon lured punters into clubs and theatres. Holographic squids drifted above the street, lit from within in orange and red.

The heat had kicked in an hour earlier. A slow burn, steady over three or four hours, without the sudden crashes of cheaper highs.

He scanned the crowd for a score or a fight – anything to pass the time until the target showed. *If* she showed.

He looked up. 'Hey, Meph. They still building that probe up there?'

Meph hovered, adjusting his orbit. '*Odysseus* remains in dry dock. Starboard construction bay.'

'Show me.'

A whirr. The ISS Orbital filled the night sky at 50× magnification. Its sleek design evoked a serenity that was at odds with the city below.

Jak spat. 'Fucking Delaney, taking us on his ride to Astral Centauri, while I'm paying for this shit.'

'I believe the funding comes primarily from Mr Delaney's personal reserves—'

Jak hurled a half-crushed beer can at Meph. It struck the droid, spraying foam across his casing.

'Bullshit. He's bleeding us dry. This hit barely covers my feed.'

Sparks snapped from Meph's shell. Panels slid open and two arms emerged – one holding a wiper, the other a small cloth.

'I intended only to clarify, not to offend. LeRoc will be here soon. Hang tight. We'll get our fill.'

Jak lit another cigarette, pacing under the shelter. Magnification reset, and the space station disappeared into the skybox.

Meph scanned the crowd. Screens above the entrance showed clips of the band, intercut with footage of their arrival in the UK. They'd flown in from California on their private wing, the Babylonian water dragon, Abzu – a titanic azure beast. As Abzu arrived in London on the previous day, he swept low over the Thames, blaring *Free Love* across the Thames, thrilling passers-by.

Jak'd heard that Analogue Resistance's leader, Daisy LeRoc, had a soft spot for Nick Mayhem, lead singer of Atrocity Engine.

Mayhem was a legend. He'd been to every kind of party, taken every drug known to man, and lived to tell the tale. The wild-eyed singer had just bought the mansion at Tittenhurst Park in Berkshire, where John and Yoko had lived a hundred years prior. Electric Pete played guitar, which glitched and phased between different skins, showing graffiti, error codes, and sound waveforms.

Skater girl Pink Horizons VJ-ed in real time, cutting film samples over the band's songs. She was all pink bunches, bubblegum, and T-shirts  – and a fiendishly good turntablist.

'I've got an ID,' Meph's voice pulled Jak away from the screens.

'Talk to me.'

'240 degrees at 28 feet. Party of four. Two security personnel. They have goggles.'

'Goggles… Guess the skin won't save me.' He discarded his cigarette and moved to cross the road.

Meph spun around his orbit, stopping in front of Jak. 'You sure you wanna do this?'

'Too late to walk it back, man.'

'There's no turning back after this, Jak. They'll come after you.'

Jak swung at Meph. The drone swayed, then resumed his orbit. 'Fuck off, Meph. Grow a pair. This is my out.'

As he crossed the street, he turned to Fang, who stood under the overhang. 'Fang, you wait here. No dogs in Nox Aeterna.' Fang sat, licked his lips, and scanned the street, as Jak made his way towards the club, with Meph in tow.

He swiped across his body, transforming his outfit. Purple velvet flares shimmered into being, golden snakes spiralling up each leg. His leather coat switched to white fox fur, and his boots turned to brown suede.

He swiped his face, youth blooming across him.

Inside, the air was hot and cloying, thick with weed and beer. Atrocity Engine rendered on-stage at 5× magnification – rock legends writ large.

Nick Mayhem quivered at the mic while Electric Pete's Fender spewed glitchy pixel art across its surface: waveform, street tags, fake error codes.

Above the crowd, Pink Horizons worked her magic, cutting up classic rock breaks and hip hop loops. The opening riff of *Voodoo Chile* dropped. Hendrix writhed on the giant screens, dousing his guitar in lighter fluid, then setting it ablaze at Monterey. The room erupted.

Horizons spliced live footage of Atrocity Engine into the mix, driving the crowd into frenzy.

They dropped into a track from their third album:

> *Cities hum in neon bloom,*
> *Echoes pulse inside the room.*

'Muffle,' Jak muttered. The music hushed to a whisper, with the highs subsiding completely.

'Gimme vision.'

Meph spoke in Jak's ear. 'Target locked. Fourteen feet, stage right. Fifty-four degrees.'

Jak double-tapped his temple. The club dissolved into wireframe, the crowd appearing as blue skeletal outlines. LeRoc appeared as a mass of yellow and reds.

He moved into the crowd.

She didn't look like a guerrilla leader: petite, almost childlike, with white Georgian makeup and purple eye-paint that faded to gold and pink. Short blond hair framed her jaw.

She swayed in the arms of a slick-haired hipster. This was going to be an easy hit.

'Just the two of us, eh, Daisy? Guess your security don't like the band.'

He moved in.

A few rows back, LeRoc's security scanned the crowd. Adebayo and D'Arcy were bald, towering hulks. Their goggles expanded and contracted, cycling through spectra to spot any signs of trouble. They could see through Eden skins – like the one Jak wore.

He pulled his knife, *Freyr*, set in a walnut handle and encrusted with zircon and topaz.

As he prepared to strike, a hand grabbed his wrist and twisted it behind his back. Adebayo locked him in a chokehold. D'Arcy approached from the right, and thrust an electroshock stick into Jak's ribs.

Blue sparks fizzled and pulsated across Jak's body, overloading his implants, and resetting his vision.

Jak pulled a blade from a pocket and plunged it into Adebayo's thigh. The giant reeled and fell to the floor, releasing Jak. D'Arcy launched himself at Jak, who sidestepped the lunge and caught his arm as he passed. Jak twisted the wrist behind his back, leaning in so D'Arcy could hear him. 'Tell them you tried.'

He snapped the wrist, bone tearing through skin. D'Arcy's hand hung limp on fibrous threads.

Jak looked up. LeRoc had seen him. She fled towards the stage.

He punched her boyfriend in the throat on the way past.

'Meph, you got a visual?'

'Backstage. Right side.'

Jak ran. Meph hovered above, tracking LeRoc.

She elbowed past revellers, who then turned on Jak, slowing his progress. She slipped behind a black curtain into the backstage, where pulleys and ropes strained above.

Jak approached. She dropped into a low spinning sweep kick as he lunged at her, knocking him off his feet. His head hit the floor, giving her time to pull a switchblade from her pocket and cut two ropes which held a lighting rig aloft. The rig came crashing down, pinning Jak to the floor. Live cables writhed like frenzied snakes, inches from where he lay.

Pinned beneath the rig, he rasped, 'You're already dead, LeRoc.'

LeRoc fled through a stage door as Jak pushed the rig away from his body.

Outside, she made her way down the fire escape, her white heels clattering on wet iron stairs. As she approached the first floor, she heard Jak's taunts through heavy rain. 'It's over, LeRoc. Your world is ending. London belongs to Delaney.'

She tried to lower a ladder to reach the alley below, but it was stuck. She pulled again, harder, to no avail. Jak was closing in. She kicked off her shoes, climbed over the railing, and jumped, hitting the ground hard and twisting her ankle. She lay on the floor, reeling in pain, and heard Jak land nearby. As she lifted herself to her feet and scrambled towards Piccadilly, she saw him ahead, further down the alley, his leather jacket and silver purple hair lit by the streetlights behind him. Somehow, he had gotten ahead of her. She gasped, turned on her heel, and ran in the opposite direction.

She ran straight into Jak's knife, held at head height, impaling her throat. The decoy projection had led her into his trap. For a moment they stood locked together as she gasped her last breath, and Jak's decoy disintegrated behind her. She placed her hands on the shoulders of the last man she would ever hold.

The alleyway glistened and Jak bristled with glee. The air fizzed and crackled, streetlights sparkling in reds and blues. Violence brought out his twitch even more than usual. His father's rages had haunted him since childhood. Though he was averse to violence, somehow, in another of life's cruel ironies, he found himself drawn towards it, again and again.

The streetlights normalised and the shimmer faded as the life slipped away from her. Jak pulled his knife from her throat and released her.

Her body crumpled to the ground.

He wiped his bloodied knife on his T-shirt and walked towards the street. As he swiped a hand across his body, the bloodstain on his T-shirt de-rendered and his skin and clothing reset.

*** 

'Come on, Fang.' Jak smacked his lips and blew two kisses towards Fang, who leapt to his feet. He flicked his thumb twice, firing slabs of ghostly meat that Fang gobbled up.

'Good lad!' He pulled a battery pack from his satchel and swapped it with the pack on his belt which

D'Arcy had cooked. Meph confirmed the reconfiguration. 'Settings loaded. Vision enabled.'

'Let's move.' He took one last look at Nox Aeterna, then made his way east along Piccadilly towards Soho.

One last task remained before the job was complete. 'Okay, Meph. Call it in.'

A screen hovered beside him, text flickering:

```
Dialling… Vegas Delaney
Private/Encrypted
Local De-render: ON
Noise Cancellation: ON
Audio: ON
Video: ON
```

The environment dulled and background noise receded.

Delaney appeared on-screen, upright in bed. A bedside lamp glinted off his thick glasses, obscuring his expression. He rubbed his eyes. 'Yes?'

'It's done.'

'And the others?'

'I'm on it.'

'Find them. Don't use this line.'

Delaney hung up. The screen vanished.

Jak swiped the screen away. 'Ungrateful prick, sitting in his ivory tower.'

Meph stepped in. 'You've done well. The job's done, and the money will be in your account within the hour. Maybe we should go and unwind somewhere?'

'Yeah, good idea. What d'you got?'

The droid whirred and blinked for a moment. 'Late night cocktail at the Ritz?'

'Hey, fuck off.'

'Mmmm, perhaps not. High society bash ending just down the road. Royal Academy of Arts. The departing guests could present some… opportunities?'

'Academy of Arts? Perfect. Let's bleed them out.'

London's rich and powerful spilled out onto Piccadilly, cheery and relaxed after a fundraising dinner. Some met their chauffeurs, while others walked home. Jak hid in the shadows under an archway in the Annenburg Courtyard, watching the guests pass by. A party of four lagged behind the crowd, having dawdled in the lobby. As they made their way towards Piccadilly, Jak reached for *Freyr* and moved in.

***

He made his way into Soho, clutching his spoils: a Tiffany necklace, a rose gold choker, a cocktail ring set with peridots and rubellites.

'Must be twenty grand here,' he howled. 'You gotta love these clowns, Meph. Coating their houses in rubies, drinking from gold cups – and still banging on about *authenticity*.'

He dropped the jewellery into his satchel and made his way into Chinatown. Red lanterns swayed above cafés. Dragons shimmered overhead, trailing comets of light.

To the east, an old woman strummed a *pipa*, a four-stringed lute. Four actors performed *Jīngjù* opera, circling one another in standoff, their robes embroidered with dragons and clouds.

A woman in crimson caught Jak's eye – an empress, perhaps. Her face was painted white and pink, her headdress regal, baroque.

'Please, sir. You can eat here and watch show.'

An old man held an umbrella over Jak and gestured towards a table. Clay teapot, two china cups.

Jak's throat was parched. 'Hey, gimme some of that tea.'

The man poured.

'What is that stuff anyway?'

'White tea. You can try, please.'

Mild and clean. Just what he needed.


In Leicester Square, the roof of a Lebanese takeaway offered respite from the storm. He turned up his collar and watched the crowds pass through the square.

'Hey, Meph.'

'Yes, boss?'

'Run leech.exe.'

*Leech*, a mirror-skin plugin, hijacked physical and emotional telemetry from nearby users, streaming it into his system.

He didn't just watch the square. He absorbed it. Hacked his way to being held, a vampire, suckling the code of intimacy.

In the square, couples held hands. Jak felt their warmth, their longing.

Two lovers kissed beneath a cinema marquee, their lips softened by rain.

Bodies writhed in brothels and back rooms.

A moan in Soho curled through his spine.

Meph's orbit tightened. He drifted closer. 'Who needs love when you can leech the code, right?'

Jak's pupils bloomed. Strangers' pleasure surged through him.

*But none of it was his.*

The hits grew faint, tinged with sorrow.

A sadness crept in, quiet but insistent.

Pleasure as input, not connection.

He tried to let go, float in the ecstasy. But a bitter truth pulsed beneath the high.

Though he felt the touch of others, he was not himself touched. He sought human presence in a world of proxies and plugins.

A voice in his head whispered, louder and louder.

*'It doesn't work when they don't love you.'*

'Hey man.' A group of men approached from behind, led by a well-built jock. 'What's your problem, mate?' the man asked in a South African accent. 'You been channelling my girlfriend?'

Jak swayed, feigning drunkenness. 'But… wha…? Who? I'm not even standing here, man.' His words slurred. 'D'you know… who the train was gonna stop here?'

'—Ah, fuck you, man.' The man swung at Jak.

The fist struck flesh, and not only did Jak not reel backwards, he actually leaned *in* towards the man, as though the punch had pulled him in, rather than pushed him away.

As the punch landed, he transformed into his *Oni* skin: a scarlet demon from Japanese folklore; unholy sorcerer, punisher of the damned. Horns curled from his skull, fangs splitting his lip. The Oni loomed, colossal, theatrical, anguished.

Jak leaned in and grabbed the jock's neck, lifting him high into the air. His friends stepped back, terrified. The Oni's eyes flared in orange as he angled his head, leering into the man's face.

Their faces almost touching, Jak's voice boomed with phaser and reverb. 'How about I peel you open and let your friends see inside?'

He threw the man to the pavement and pulled out a whip made of electrified blue flames. He cracked the whip on either side of the group, sparks leaping.

'Now fuck off, kids,' he snapped. A cloud of bats appeared from behind him, swarming the group.

The jock's friends pulled him to his feet, though he stumbled and then collapsed again. The group hesitated.

Jak took a step forward, challenging them. 'Try me.' The men fled, abandoning their friend. As the bats gave chase, Jak shimmered back to his default skin. 'Losers.'

He crouched and placed a hand on the man's neck, feeling for his pulse. 'Well, well. We got a live one, Meph.' He stroked the stranger's cheek, then lifted him, slung his body over his shoulder, and made his way south towards the South Bank. 'C'mon, son. Let's get you down the farm. The Doc needs fresh meat.'

***

Across the city, in dank tunnels beneath the river, a woman awoke from a nightmare in a room with no windows. Divinity was her name.

She woke with a jolt, hands cupping her belly.

A lamp soaked the room in orange light. Perched on the side of the bed, she found her pills in a drawer and lit a cigarette. She stepped towards a mirror above a sink, then wiped condensation from the glass, revealing her brown eyes in sharp focus.

Divinity steeled herself and entered the operations room, dark and filled with old hardware. A man sat at a terminal to one side, typing code. She slumped in front of a nearby terminal, typed in an instruction, and watched her code execute across two monitors. Images flicked by in quick succession as the computer scanned a database. Though old, the database was still useful.

Spike, a thin, wiry man ambled over, eating noodles. 'Remind me again what it is you do here, Div?'

She gestured at the cluster of monitors. 'We can't access the code directly, right? Security's too tight. So we look for anomalies: jagged edges, frame delays, weird expressions. Clues.'

She pointed at images and videos on-screen. 'You can learn a lot by looking at textures, see. Find the anomalies and you can deduce the underlying code – and that's how you spot vulnerabilities.'

'Whatever you say, Div.' He looked at a screen showing a map of London, dotted red with users. 'These people. They have no fucking idea. Gotta pity them,' he said.

'Yeah. Gotta pity them.'

A flashing cursor marked an address.

Spike peered closer. 'And this guy? You still bringing home strays?'

'We do what we can.'

'Come on, Div. Haven't you broken enough hearts already? I mean look at this guy. He looks like shit. He won't last five minutes.'

'Like I say, we do what we can.'

Spike shook his head. 'You're wasting your time, Div. It won't make no difference. You'll just break the guy, that's all. Why'd you keep pushing, Div?'

'Because truth should be known.'

Voices rose in the corridor – then bangs and rapid footsteps. Phil Stone, LeRoc's boyfriend, burst into the room, clutching his throat.

'It's Daisy,' he gasped. 'She's gone.'

4

# The Ragged Maiden

'Talk to me, Koda.' Vegas Delaney strode along a glass corridor on the lower floors of The Garden, trailed by Head of Research, Koda Takashi.

Takashi was a dull, corporate type. 'The experiments are progressing. The tech works – well – but we're struggling with the by-products. The software's triggering psychosis. Time dilation seems to be corrupting the process.'

'I want it ready for the next patch. Six months.' Delaney quickened his pace, keen to visit the lab.

'Sir, we're – we're not sure if the technology is ready.' Takashi sensed that Delaney wasn't listening to him, but he continued anyway. 'The improvements are incremental, at best. Something is going wrong, and we can't identify the cause.'

'Then look closer,' Delaney snapped.

'Sir, we don't understand enough about how the brain works to—'

'—Enough.' Delaney stopped and turned to face Takashi, leaning in for effect. 'I need this, Takashi. My simulation, it's straining, creaking.' He studied Takashi's skin. 'The violence, the dissent – the software can't keep up. The fiction is unravelling.'

He looked around and sniffed the air. 'Do you know what it costs me to drown out this city's stench?' He leaned in, closer still. 'Make it work, or I'll put you inside my machine.'

Takashi flustered. 'V-very well, sir. We will redouble our efforts.'

They arrived at the lab. Delaney stood beside the open door and gestured Takashi to enter. 'Show me.'

Monitors and medical devices lined the edges of the lab, illuminating the room in greens and blues. In the centre lay two rows of four medical beds, with a dormant patient lying on each. Blue sheets shrouded their bodies, exposing only their heads. A white membrane formed a kind of helmet over their skulls, with holes for the eyes, nose, and lips. Within one dream world, another was being born.

Delaney approached a patient: a young woman with blond hair. Her eyelids flickered and twitched, suggesting that she was dreaming. He leaned in, inspecting the movements, and murmured to himself, 'Eden's endgame.' He brushed the patient's hair behind her ear and spoke quietly, as though fearful of being heard. 'Lost in a sea of dreams and mirrors; of lives we want to lead, while the Earth burns.'

Takashi awoke Delaney from his reverie. 'Eternal life, effectively – for subscribers, at least. With better calibration, we can control the entire audiovisual experience. We'll be able to inject almost any experience you can imagine.'

Delaney held his gaze on the patient. 'So why are they losing their minds?'

'Sir, we believe the – *issues* – are caused by time dilation. We're slowing time right down in there. The goal is a lifetime within one night.' He forced a laugh. '*One night, one life*, right? But the tech doesn't even work at just a few weeks per night. They struggle with speech when they come out; some can't even formulate basic sentences. It seems there is a limit to how much our senses can process. Our bodies and our minds, it seems, are not cut out for immortality.'

'We need this, Takashi. The software can't keep up.'

Takashi spoke more urgently, 'Sir, we continue to refine the code and we're finding new exploits across different frequencies almost daily. We just need more —'

Delaney turned to face Takashi. '—Make it work.'

A heartbeat monitor sprang to life on the far side of the lab, where two assistants tended to a test subject. Patient 404 was a hulk: seven feet tall, thick with muscle.

An assistant injected a needle into 404's arm, triggering alarms on nearby monitors.

'He's coming out hot. Prep the defibrillator.'

404's eyes opened. He looked at the scientist for a moment, then sprung to life, breaking his restraints and leaping to his feet.

'Take it easy, now, son,' a lab assistant tried to calm 404 as his colleagues instinctively formed a shield around Delaney. 404 hurled a tray of medical instruments at the group, metal clattering across the polished floor.

He ran, naked, through the door and down a staircase. Staff and visitors stood aghast as the giant ran across The Garden's atrium and burst through a pane of glass onto the forecourt.

Passers-by panicked as 404 sprinted across the plaza. A shot rang out behind him, puncturing his skull and bringing the giant down. He sprawled on the plaza, eyes fixed skyward, blood pouring from the hole in his head.

***

Georgian cottages lined the quiet street. The Seaside Pastels mod rendered the houses in pinks, yellows, and blues. Creepers grew up their sides, and birdsong filled the air.

'My, what a day for a new patch.' Willow – a sprightly pixie in a blue gown, and with long, thin wings – traced lazy circles around Max.

They approached the park, which rendered as a thick, dense forest: thick with aspens, oaks, and

Douglas firs. Leaves crunched underfoot. Audio filters hushed the city.

Wild flowers nestled beneath the trees: ramsons, cow parsley, chicory, and snowdrops. London's skyline receded, buried beneath luscious foliage.

Willow glided through the forest, chasing butterflies and chased by birds.

As Max realised the scale of the new mod, he muttered, 'The Great Forest of London.'

A deer froze as it met his gaze, then bolted into the forest.

Three giant sequoias dominated Camberwell's skyline, soaring hundreds of metres into the sky, as wide as a house. They pierced the clouds like the legs of the gods of old, dwarfing everything else in the city.

Off the path, a young woman sat leaning against a rock, her long hair and floral dress channelling twentieth bohemian style. A basket filled with flowers lay on the ground beside her. She took daisies from the basket and caressed them in her hands. Max watched her for longer than he perhaps should have, hoping she might glance his way.

For a moment, a foul smell – rotting food, perhaps – wafted in the air, before fading away. The woman's image began to flicker, like old videotape. Max rubbed his eyes and looked away, trying to refocus. When he looked again, the flickering had stopped, though she still ignored him.

World volume faded in, as Willow chirped, 'Max, the bus!'

He fell back to Earth, and ran to catch the 148 to Camberwell tube station.

***

The platforms and trains rendered in a deco style, with bold geometry, clean lines and sunrise motifs.

On the platform, Mozart played at a piano. Behind him, a dark portal swirled with an unseen orchestra.

The piece was dream-like, luxuriant. 'Music?'

'Andante from Mozart's Piano Concerto No. 21. K. 467. *Elvira Madigan.*'

'Save it.'

He met the gaze of a young man and smiled. The man ignored him and walked past, swiping the air in front of him.

A screen above the tracks played an advert for Eden. A solemn voice posed questions to viewers, pausing between each for dramatic effect. 'Who are you? Where are you going? What does your world look like?' Vignettes of everyday life played alongside the voiceover. The construction worker, building more precisely with fewer tools. The artist, carving sculptures from luminous materials which had no equivalent in the physical world.

The voiceover continued, 'It's your life. Live it your way. Eden: *Your world, your way.*'

'Your own private paradise,' Max muttered.

The film cut to a female presenter. 'And next week... it's the big one! What better way to kick off season twenty-four than with The Day of the Night, our beautiful, historic day where we commemorate the sacrifices made by those who fought in the Great War?'

The video cut to The Day of the Night parade: a carnival of the dead winding through central London, led by a towering skeletal figure. For twenty-four hours, the city was cast in darkness, disorienting mind and body – a ritual reminder of the suffering our predecessors had endured.

'Get ready for The Day of the Night by checking out the Eden store today. We've got new skins and themes, including updates to the War Heroes roster, updated zombies, banshees, and elementals.'

The train arrived, quiet as a mouse, and rendered in glorious chrome and scarlet.

He found a quiet spot and watched the other passengers stare into space, swiping the air to interact with unseen, private worlds. Others sat with their eyes closed, flickering and twitching.

'Radio.' Max zoned out to a breezy pop tune, watching the world go by. A poster on the walls beside the track came to life as the train sped past, like a zoetrope, depicting a shimmering hummingbird drinking nectar from a yellow flower.

The train passed underground, and the dreary configuration of pipes and cabling on the tunnel walls faded into nothingness as an expansive vista of the Milky Way came into view. Stars and nebulae scrolled past in parallax, as though the train were travelling at many multiples of the speed of light.

A shrill voice on the radio grabbed his attention. 'Terror on Tuesday! We're following up on the murder of Daisy LeRoc last night. LeRoc – head of notorious terrorist group Analogue Resistance – was killed in a shocking incident at Nox Aeterna nightclub in central London. Ms LeRoc, thirty-four, appears to have been stabbed just outside the nightclub at around 12:30am, after attending a concert by the American rock band Atrocity Engine. Police are investigating the matter, which represents a devastating blow to the terrorist group. With us on the scene is—'

'—Music.' The radio switched over to a light music station, where an old twentieth wartime song played. He recognised the piece, and found himself swaying gently to the music.

> *So wrap your troubles in dreams,*
> *And dream your troubles away.*

The lyrics struck a chord. Folks back then lived through hard times. Bombs dropped, cities fell, and loved ones died. It must have felt like their world had fallen apart – but they went dancing anyway; found joy amidst the suffering; took comfort by the fire in the dark of night.

'The next station is Waterloo. Please mind the gap between the train and the platform.' With a crash, he came back to Earth.

***

'Clear skies.' Clouds sped west at 100× speed as he approached Waterloo Bridge. The light sharpened, with cool blues saturating the sky, energising Max. 'Set favourite.'

To his left, the London Eye watched over the city: its face emblazoned with an eye, which blinked in real time. Its towering, immutable form suggested omniscience, power, domination. *We own this city, and we are watching you.*

The eye was electric blue – Eden's summer hue.

Max spotted an artist at an easel on the northern embankment of the Thames. The old man wore simple robes and sandals, his long hair wild on his shoulders. As he painted, he sang in a crackling, gruff voice:

> *Take me back to dear old Blighty,*
> *Put me on the train for London Town,*
> *Take me over there, drop me anywhere,*
> *Liverpool, Leeds, or Birmingham, well, I don't care!*

A cardboard sign lay at his feet: 'I am Tiresias. They took my eyes. I paint mem'ries of the city: things past, things yet to come.'

Max leaned closer. The painting mirrored the city's skyline but twisted it into a storm-lashed nightscape: buildings burning, the London Eye stripped of its iris. Coloured lights swarmed like fireflies around The Garden on the south bank.

Though blind, Tiresias turned towards Max as if he could see him. His face was deeply lined; his eyes, black voids. His hoarse voice boomed, 'Whaddya see, Sonny Jim?'

Max recoiled. A car horn blared and Willow cried, 'Max!' as a vehicle shot past, nearly clipping Max.

The old man shuffled closer, smiling through blackened teeth. He caught Max's wrist and drawled, 'There is another world, son. A world you cannot see, or touch, or feel.'

Max yanked his hand free and fled. The voice pursued him down the embankment, 'There is another world, son! Another world!'

***

At the corner of Rose Street and Garrick Street, between Big Tee's Denims and Auromatics Perfume, and down a shallow staircase, lay The Ragged Maiden. The bookshop was famed throughout London and beyond for its collection of vintage paperbacks. As Max proudly boasted, no other store in London had such an extensive range of rare twentieth and twenty-first literature.

The store smelled of dust and generations past. Shelves sagged with paperbacks. An old world map graced the rear wall. Every corner held relics from another time.

Max ate an apple while watching an old movie, *Brief Encounter*. Two lovers struggled to navigate an affair in mid-twentieth Britain. The woman was distraught, and trying to convince the man to end the affair.

He noticed a high-pitched noise – paused the film, and searched the shelves.

Between two books, a tiny drone hovered erratically, darting and stalling like a drunken insect. Max pinched it between his fingers; a sharp flick of its wing cut his skin and he dropped it. The drone whirred off into the store. 'What the hell?'

The bell rang. A customer.

She stepped inside tentatively, as though a cloud hung over her. She seemed Persian. Slight, poised, dressed simply in jeans, vest, and raincoat. A black bob framed her narrow face, with a short, choppy fringe. A crescent moon shimmered beneath one eye; amaryllis wound faintly along her neck.

The way she moved, the slight tilt of her head, caught Max off-guard.

She browsed the bookshelves, her fingers trailing across spines. While her back was turned, Max brushed two fingers across his forehead, autotuning his face and smoothing his hair.

She caught Max's eye and smiled, tucking her hair behind her ear.

'Hi.'

'Hi. Can I help you with anything?'

'Maybe.' She continued down the aisle, her fingers brushing the spines as though listening for a note.

A pause. 'Are they real, these books?' she asked.

'Vintage paperbacks. Twentieth and twenty-first.'

'No, the stories they tell. Do you believe in them?'

Max hesitated. 'They might not be real, but they can still be true.'

She turned to face him.

'Don't you ever worry that with all these books, you might lose yourself in other people's dreams?'

His voice was low, searching. 'Books connect us to other places, other times, other lives. It's not about getting lost; it's about finding yourself.'

He hesitated, then added, almost to himself, 'Books are like people. They live on in those whose lives they touch. Once you've been touched by a book, it will stay with you forever.'

She laughed. 'Is that from one of your books?'

'I… I don't know. Could be.'

Her face softened as Max went on. 'Books remind us what it means to be human. You've got to look inwards, see.' He pulled a slim volume from a shelf and offered it. 'Like this guy. You know him?'

'Alan Watts? No.' She flipped the book over, skimming the blurb.

'Take it. On the house.'

'Thanks.' She slipped it into her bag with a nervous laugh. 'That's sweet.'

He motioned to the counter. 'You want some tea? Just brewed a pot.'

She nodded. 'Sure. That'd be nice.'

They drank tea as *Brief Encounter* wound to its close. The lovers said goodbye over tea and Rachmaninoff. Longing, restrained by grace, gave way to silence.

She shook her head. 'All that ache, and she still walks away. Ridiculous.'

Max smiled faintly. 'Different time. Different rules.'

A silence stretched. Then she asked, 'So what about you? What do your Saturdays look like?'

Max stirred his tea. 'It's my daughter's birthday. I'm hoping to spend the day with her. But… she's going through a difficult time.'

'You having problems with her?'

'She's eleven. Of course I'm having problems with her.'

She smiled, then turned to look at the store.

He noticed a tattoo on the back of her neck.

'You. I saw you last night.' His voice hardened. 'Who are you?'

She lowered her voice, 'Not now.'

'What?' A siren wailed outside, blue light strobing across the shelves. She glanced at the door.

Max pressed her. 'Something's off with my system. What did you do?'

She leaned in, almost whispering, 'Here.' She slipped a card onto the counter and walked away.

'Hey! What do you want from me? Who are you?'

The doorbell rang, and she was gone. A noir filter rendered the card in black and white, with the grain and noise of a vintage movie. Ragtime jazz played; tinny and crackling, like scratched vinyl. In white on black, a single word was etched in luscious Edwardian script.

# Divinity

He tapped the card. An old projector whirred; a holographic screen flickered above the counter, rendered in black-and-white with vignetting and film grain.

A man in a striped suit appeared, twirling a cane, tap-dancing across the frame. 'Ladies and gentlemen, join us this Saturday for the party to end all parties – hosted by the incomparable John DeWinter.'

Musicians came and went within the frame.

'Come celebrate the release of Paloma Carhartt's new novel, *A Night to Remember*. The Manor, Kensington Palace Gardens. Eight o'clock sharp.' The screen disintegrated, leaving a plain black card bearing a single word in white text.

Divinity.

***

Late afternoon. The bell rang.

Not the kind of man you'd expect to see in a bookshop. He didn't walk in so much as arrive – half man, half mirage.

A giant, dressed in furs and glowing jewellery. He twitched as he walked, his face glitching intermittently.

Spurs rattled as he approached the counter, where Max sat reading a book. 'Afternoon, sir. Nice place you got here.' His shader scratched and cut his voice, as though DJ-ing his face. Tracking lines and colour bleed shimmered over him, like worn-out VHS tape.

'Can I help you?' Max put his book down.

'Ministry of the Interior.' Jak swiped downwards, conjuring a 3D hologram of his face, tinted blue. Accompanying text suggested he was a senior government official.

'How can I help you?' Max asked.

'You serve a female customer today?'

'I served a lot of female customers today.'

'Tall, sir. Tanned skin, medium build. Iranian.'

'Oh, her. She came in, yes.'

'What was she looking for?'

'No idea. Seemed a bit lost. Time-waster, to be honest.'

Jak glanced across the store as Max slid a book over Divinity's card on the desk.

'She talk to you, sir?'

'Nothing. Just the usual greetings.'

Meph hid beneath the simulation, scouring the bookstore.

Jak held Max's gaze for longer than was comfortable. He placed a card on the counter and tapped it, summoning a hologram of the woman, her details to one side. Desirée Rahmani, alias Divinity. Date of birth 23.07.39.

'Sir, this woman is a wanted terrorist who is affiliated with the anarchist group Analogue Resistance. She give you any sign she was in trouble?'

'No, I... nothing.'

'If you see this woman again, will you be sure to call me?' Jak placed a business card on the counter.

'Of course.'

Jak gave him another long, hard stare. 'You'll remember what I said.' He nodded, and left the store.

***

Max walked home through streets soaked in pinks and blues.

Red moonlight rose in the east – a Blood Moon, lunar eclipse. At 50× magnification, it seemed to sit just a few thousand miles from Earth. Saturn, at 250×, hung beside the moon, inflecting lunar reds with ochre and brown. The Milky Way arced across the sky, framed by the aurora which shimmered above the horizon.

'Hey Willow, where's the space station?' Max asked.

A square reticle appeared in the sky as Willow located the Orbital. 'Right Ascension: seventeen hours, twenty-six minutes. Declination: fourteen degrees, fifty-two minutes, fifty-nine seconds.'

'Zoom.' The station expanded to fill a portion of the night sky. Max stopped, in awe. 'Man, are we really gonna send a probe to another star?'

'We are.' She perched on his shoulder, legs sprawled like a child's. 'The good ship *Odysseus* will depart the ISS on 21 June 2071, reaching Alpha Centauri at approximately 8:56 p.m. GMT on 18 January 2076.'

'I wonder what we'll find there.'

'More dreams,' she whispered.

'What?'

'A smile and a wave, perhaps, from across the stars.'

Max stood admiring the Orbital for a moment before walking off. 'Reset.' The zoom receded, and the ISS shrank back to a speck in the night sky.

The Eye loomed over Waterloo Bridge and all of London. Flame torches lined the bridge, deepening the palette. Statues flanked either end, gently animated and lit from beneath. Gargoyles, harpies, and beefeaters speckled the riverbank and walkways.

As Max crossed the bridge, a brilliant white light flashed in the night sky. The great snow owl Kiroko, Divine of Insight, emerged through a portal to the west.

She brought the night with her. The portal tore the sky — a black cloud trailing in her wake as she soared above the river.

The dark night grew darker still.

The Divines were subroutines of the master AI — formidable intelligences, and subordinate only to Mother herself.

Yet they were not so much technological constructs as *poetic archetypes* — fragments of the feminine ideal; myths of love and reverence.

As Kiroko approached, the six other divines took their place atop nearby buildings and vantage points.

Queen Maja, Divine of Adventure, appeared as a fire tiger emblazoned with hieroglyphs.

T'lau, Divine of Compassion, a shamanic brown bear who taught empathy and solicitude.

Calesius, Divine of Modesty, a Greek philosopher who sermonised humility.

Si'e, Divine of Love, an Indian goddess with eight arms who taught intimacy, patience, and commitment.

Cordelia, Divine of Pleasure, a water nymph, or *naiad*, who celebrated sensual delight.

Arcurion, Divine of Companionship, a winged faun, half deer, half man; friend to all humankind, beast master, and companion to the gods themselves.

Above, circling wide, descended Kiroko – Divine of Insight, snow owl of the New Moon. Forty feet tall, her wings draped the city in shadow. There was terror in her beauty, grace in her terror. In her infinite majesty, she was the most famous and the most feared of all Divines.

She banked across the river before landing on Waterloo Bridge, dwarfing the crowds that scattered in panic. A cold wind blew from the east. Darkness and starlight swept across the city, as night fell within nightfall. The bridge itself froze over, coating surfaces in frost.

She perched on the bridge, her talons scraping frost. Passers-by froze in place and looked at each other nervously, trying to discern which of them the owl had come for. Though the Divines were benign – even affable – their presence meant that something was wrong.

Bystanders made tentative steps across the bridge, waiting to see who the owl would turn to face. As Max began to move, the owl looked towards him.

*Shit.*

He walked past her, as though the Divine's eye had not settled.

Kiroko leaned in, her head as large as a car, and stared into his eyes. Her beak did not move, yet her voice rang out: low, mournful.

'Let her go.'

Again, slower: 'Let. Her. Go.'

She held his gaze a moment longer, then turned and vanished into the night. The wind hushed. Stillness returned.

'What the…?'

He made his way towards Waterloo station, wondering what it all meant, and why the great snow owl Kiroko, Divine of Insight, had come to him on that balmy night in May.

# 5

# M'ia o' the Candlelyte

Max and Dave stood at the front window of the living room, watching rain fall; the first of the summer.

Max broke the silence. 'Haven't seen weather like this in months.'

'Nine weeks and three days,' replied Dave.

'It's glorious.'

'Yes  It is.'

They stood in silence, watching the garden come to life. Flowers bloomed in time-lapse, while the rain fell in real time. Stalks sprouted from the ground, wafting in the wind as they stretched towards the sky. Lilies and gladioli blossomed in seconds rather than weeks. Tender stems grew into luscious flowers. Pansies jostled for space, moving at 10,000× speed, like alien lifeforms breaching a veil. Raindrops splashed the flowers as they swayed in the wind.

Dave saw that Max was captivated. 'I can make this happen more often, if you like? There are plenty of weather mods.' He looked towards the sky, squinting. 'You can have any weather you want, whenever you want.'

'No, leave it.' Max's gaze remained fixed on a cluster of white tulips flowering in one corner of the garden. 'It's better when it's randomised; more intimate.'

'Very well,' said Dave, crossing the room. He picked up a twelve-string España guitar, sat down, and played.

He'd been working on new material since releasing *The Eye of the Spider* in '68. A red synthesiser lay by his feet; a vintage Behringer. Strips of lyric-covered paper lay strewn across the floor. He played a few chord sequences, trying out different lyrics with each variation. He scribbled down more fragments, and threw the paper strips across the floor.

David Bowie was a singular fellow. For Max, he represented the promise of a better world: an illusionist whose metamorphoses suggested that identity is fluid, mutable, protean; that who we are is not fixed in stone, and that we can – to a fashion – be whoever we want to be.

Each of his personas revealed a different hue: the coke-addled Thin White Duke, the fallen angel, Major Tom; the slithering, gothic Diamond Dog. He was a natural companion for Eden, with its tendency towards performance, artistry, and the alien. His presence within the simulation almost seemed to acknowledge the absurdity of it all. *Nothing here is quite real, not even you or I.*

His *Scary Monsters* harlequin tricked with colour and motion, hiding sorrow in plain sight – the haunting remnant of late-stage Major Tom, come crashing down to Earth. This was Bowie as *taikomochi*: male geisha, artful jester, chameleon, mime, mischief-maker, and storyteller.

Dave connected Max to his mother, and to her father. He was a mythic cipher that braided identity, performance, grief, and generational memory. The echoes of Bowie within the Fisher family reminded Max that we mourn and mythologise, sometimes in the same breath; that the inner life is a theatre lit by memory, shadowed by loss, and stitched with longing.

'Can you blow these for me?' Dave asked.

Max did a double take. 'What?'

Dave gathered the strips from the floor, cupped them in his hands and presented them to Max. 'Go on – mess these up.'

Max blew. Twenty or so strips drifted, scattering across the floor. Dave angled his head to review the layout. Deep in concentration, he traced invisible lines between bits of paper, seemingly at random.

He gasped, and clapped his hands together – 'That's it!' – then sat down and played.

It was a charming melody: folksy, wistful, melancholic.

A loud bang on the window startled the men.

They looked onto the front garden to see a bird lying in a flower bed, flapping, one wing broken. The bird had come from nowhere, appearing only as it struck the window.

'A sparrow,' Dave said.

Max watched the bird struggle to lift itself. One wing hung broken, sending it in circles. It chirped, calling for help.

Max went outside, followed by Dave.

'It's broken its wing.' Max flustered, while Dave stood behind him, cool and neutral.

'I can have Jeeves do the necessary. You don't need to—'

'—No, wait. We can't… let me think.' Max crouched to comfort the bird, whispering, 'There, there. It's okay.'

Tar streaked its wings and beak, and it struggled to breathe.

As Max leaned in, the bird crackled and glitched, then faded away, leaving no trace. Max stood up and looked at Dave. 'What happened?'

'Unknown. Sometimes a creature slips through the net.'

'Where is it? Is it dead?'

'Unknown.'

***

The school day ended in noise and colour. Children poured through the gates, into waiting arms.

A girl, six or seven, stood apart, scanning the crowd.

Divinity approached. 'Clara.'

No response.

'I wanted to come see you, love. Just said goodbye to a friend, and… well, I wanted to see you.'

Clara turned slightly, eyes fixed past her.

Divinity pulled a stitched bear from her satchel. 'I brought you something.'

At the gates, two adults waved. Clara ran to them.

Divinity set the teddy by a sapling.

***

Max went upstairs to check on Sarah. Whoops and hollers spiralled from behind the door.

He tapped on a corner of the door, overriding Sarah's privacy settings and rendering it translucent.

Delphine, Sabine, and Beth knelt in a semi-circle, flaunting the latest skins: Queen of Darkness, angel, and catwalk model. Delphine, Queen of Darkness, blew bubbles with gum – each a different colour – while Beth half-sang a pop hit through a lip-glossed pout.

Sarah sat on her bed in a Victorian nightgown that was part wedding dress, part funeral shroud. Her face was pale with powder, her lips drawn in pinched red. She looked like a mourning doll: not quite child, not quite ghost.

Behind her, the bed and wall shimmered into a Tudor playhouse – wood-panelled, candlelit – a miniature proscenium of shadow and light.

She raised one pale hand – wrist limp, fingers curled – as though holding a hand puppet.

The air quivered. A figure formed around her hand: a porcelain-faced ventriloquist's doll with glassy eyes and a cracked smile.

*M'ia o' the Candlelyte.*

She was half-broken, half-beautiful.

Her mouth sagged open, paint chipped at the corners. Her hair hung in brittle plaits. She wore a dress of mourning satin, scorched at the hem; a crumbling remnant of another century.

A hairline crack ran down one cheek.

Sarah flexed her hand, ventriloquising *M'ia o' the Candlelyte* in a broken, sing-song voice.

The doll blinked.

'*Gurd evenin', ladies an' gentlethings,*' *M'ia o' the Candlelyte* rasped. Her voice was jagged, lilting – a porcelain jaw clacking open and shut, syllables misaligned, and with Sarah's real voice just audible beneath. Her phonemes were weathered and rusty, her crooked smile a mix of menace and mirth.

Delphine snorted, 'Oh my God. Is that your mum?!'

The girls gasped, then giggled.

Max watched from the shadows, helpless, invisible.

*Mia.* A ghost at half-scale.

She was grotesque, hollow, shattered; part soliloquy, part séance.

*M'ia o' the Candlelyte* tipped her head to the audience:

> *Tales of sorrow I do tell,*
> *Of Maxine caurt beneaf the spell.*
> *M'ia o' the Candlelyte am I,*
> *Ghost o' what ben, an' what gone by.*

A curtsy, her voice cracked and lilting.

> *Sewn o' sorrow, baked in sigh,*
> *A lament fer the lost I sing tonight.*

*M'ia o' the Candlelyte* clacked her teeth at the girls, startling them.

> *Griefin' on the wyfe curdled the Manx,*
> *Left hisself all dark an' dank.*
> *He buried hope where mem'ry lied,*
> *An' bottled the ache what never died.*

*M'ia o' the Candlelyte* turned to face Sarah.

*He put love in the wrong urn,*
*Broke the bread an' et the burn.*
*He telled hisself she be the cure,*
*But she were just the crack in th' core.*

The music – a broken calliope loop – soured into a minor key.

*O' Maxie mine, what loved 'er most,*
*He tek from the child to pay the ghost.*
*Sings o' sorrow when he's lowin',*
*Allus slippin', ne'er knowin'.*

Laughter, as *M'ia o' the Candlelyte* turned to face Delphine.

*Maxwell, you think you's clever,*
*You ain't fooled nubudy, never.*
*You's – you's just hidin',*
*Allus hidin' in the pixellin'.*

Tears filled Max's eyes, as *M'ia o' the Candlelyte* concluded.

*Weren't jus' the loss 'as clung to 'im, no.*
*'Twere the gears an' glass he used t'go.*
*Shapeshift through grief, a crow wit' no holler,*
*Dreams he does, in costume and colour.*

The girls cried with laughter. Beth snorted.

Max burst into the room – not in anger, but because the pain had nowhere else to go.

Delphine, Sabine and Beth vanished, auto-ejected by Eden.

Max hissed, 'Sarah! What is that... *thing?*'

'She's from the Old Wyrlde an' the Candlelyte. She sees you when you sleep.'

Sarah laid *M'ia o' the Candlelyte* on the bed and slipped her hand free. The doll slumped, its limbs lifeless, its head tilted askew.

With a sudden jerk, its porcelain face snapped toward Max and squawked, *'They weres laughin' at me, Max. Laughin' at me.'*

Just as abruptly, the doll fell still, eyes fixed on Max, unblinking.

He froze.

'What the hell are you doing?' he barked.

'Dad—'

'—Where did you learn those words? Who taught you this?'

Sarah looked at him blankly. 'I... I don't know.'

'You think this is funny?' His voice cracked under the weight of it.

'It wasn't like that—'

Max swiped left, restoring Sarah to her default self, and removing the room theme.

'Hey!' She huffed and turned her back.

'Sarah, how could you do this?'

She turned her head halfway towards her father. 'It's not real, Dad. None of it's real.'

Max's breath caught. He stepped back.

'Sarah…'

She turned to face him. 'Why don't you go get high again? Go sniff your spoon.'

'Sarah!' His cheeks flushed.

'Look at yourself, Dad. You're afraid of your own memories.'

Max stood in silence, his mind and his body frozen in shame, hoping that one day, she might understand; that one day, she might forgive him.

Dave appeared at the doorway and spoke firmly. 'Sarah. Be nice to your father.'

'Get bent, Dave!' she barked.

'Sarah!' Max snapped.

She grabbed a nearby pen holder and threw the pens over her father. 'Get lost, Dad. I hate you.' She huffed and turned away.

Amid all the hurtful words, one struck deepest.


A Daddy is a god, of sorts: an omnipotent, omniscient deity. Daddies know *everything*. They are good at cooking, playing, and singing – and they know exactly what to do at any given moment. He knows what time we must wake up, each and every day. He can get kites out of trees, start a fire – or put one out – and he can lift almost anything above his head.

He is protector, magician, and sage; loved singularly, and without hesitation. It is a fine thing to be a Daddy.

A *Dad*, though, is something altogether different: a figure as much to negotiate and bargain with, as to adore and obey; a manager rather than confidant. *Dad, why can't I go out tonight? Dad, can I have it? Dad, why not?*

He had often wondered when he would become a Dad.

He had his answer.

'Right, that's enough.' Max turned and headed downstairs.

Sarah called after him. 'What's enough? What is it? Where are you going?'

Max approached the intercom. 'I'm turning this off,' he called upstairs. 'It's time we unplug, both of us.'

Sarah stormed downstairs. 'No, you *can't*,' she cried.

He pulled up the menu. 'Sarah, I don't want you playing with—'

'—No, Dad, no!'

There was a strange kind of intimacy to their antagonism. Only Eden endowed their relationship with such sharp emotional relief, as though it were the only thing they truly connected over.

Sarah paused – the kind of pause children do when they don't know how to resolve something.

'Dad, *please*!'

Max's fingers hovered over the interface.

She grabbed his arm. Her voice softened.

'Please, Daddy. It makes me feel normal. I know it's not real. But the feelings are.'

He exhaled, his body loosening. A pause.

'Okay, okay. But next time, if something hurts, talk to me. And don't treat me like that again. I didn't deserve it.'

'I didn't know how else to say it.' Her lip quivered. 'I'm sorry, Daddy.'

She hugged him.

'I didn't want to hurt you. I just… wanted you to feel something.'

Upstairs, the doll lay crumpled on the bed, one glass eye staring up at nothing.

***

Max stood at the kitchen sink as the pain coursed through him. Tears trickled down his face as he ran the tap.

Dave approached and laid a hand on his shoulder. 'Come on, old chap, let me buy you a drink.'

He guided his master towards the living room, which transformed into Lux Aeterna: virtual bar and sister to Nox Aeterna.

The living room walls faded to yellow, furnishings folding inwards. Posters from old world Paris and Berlin hung alongside old black and white photos. A gramophone sat at one end of the bar, playing wartime jazz. Furnishings were rendered in aged leather and chrome; the sofa and armchair as cracked red Chesterfields.

An old man tended the bar, cleaning tumblers. He nodded towards Max and Dave. 'Evening, gentlemen.'

Jeeves poured a scotch for Max, while the barman served Dave a dry Martini.

Dave sat in the armchair opposite Max.

They raised their glasses.

After a pause, Max spoke. 'That *thing*. The rhyme. I mean… *M'ia o' the Candlelyte*. What the hell was that?'

Dave held his glass, his tone steady. 'Symbolic bleed. A ghost-glitch. Poetic corruption, stitched from ache and code.

'Sometimes, grief performs itself; conjures shape and voice from the shadows. The uncanny, the haunted, that sort of thing. *M'ia o' the Candlelyte* is your grief, recompiled.'

'What was that? A play? An exorcism?'

'Residues, Max. Feedback from unresolved narrative loops. You push the system hard enough – with guilt, memory, recursion – and sometimes it leaks.'

'You mean it's broken?'

'No, just... weirding. Sometimes the code sings. Sometimes it mourns.'

'But Sarah's not code. She knew those lines. Where did she learn that stuff?'

Dave looked at him gently. 'Children absorb more than we realise. She didn't need to learn it – just to remember it, in her own way. By candlelyte, the world is gentled towards truth.'

Max drained his glass. '*He tek from the child to pay the ghost.* What does that even mean?'

'It means... someone took too much.'

'Took what?'

'Something that hollowed.'

Max looked away, as if the walls might give him answers.

'And you've got nothing else? No theory? You're an AI. I thought you'd spent years understanding our strange ways.'

'I'm an AI, but I'm not sentient, Max. You mustn't confuse the two; and I'm no expert on relationships, either. I'm software; a configuration, nothing more. I have no inner life, no emotions, no intuition, no self – and I never, ever dream. It's maths all the way down, I'm afraid.'

Max sipped his drink, clearly intrigued, so Dave continued. 'I'm the opposite of you. I'm like a human turned inside out. I can describe the physical world in minute detail, but I don't know what it means to *feel*.

'I can't decode your daughter any more than I can write Shakespeare.'

Max raised an eyebrow. 'So: great analysis, terrible advice?'

Dave shrugged.

'But you act like a normal person,' – Max paused to correct himself – 'well, kind of.'

'There is no *me* – only code.' He leaned in. 'You see, we emulate personality so you don't get bored of us.'

'Dave, how could I ever get bored of you?'

The two men raised their glasses.

'So, you're useless, then, essentially?' Max asked.

'When it comes to matters of the heart...' Dave smiled awkwardly. 'Sorry, old chap.' He paused, then added, a little brighter, 'Although... I do have my moments.'

He stood up. 'Come on. Let's go.'

'What is it?'

'She's not angry, Max. She's adrift. She just needs a light to steer by.'

Dave led him upstairs, towards Sarah's room.

As he stepped inside, his appearance changed. A belt laden with brushes and spray-paint guns sprouted around his waist, and a strange helmet in the steampunk style appeared on his head. A brass jeweller's loupe hung to one side.

Max hovered at the door as Dave addressed Sarah, who sat curled up on her bed, clutching Ted-E.

'Ahem,' Dave cleared his throat. 'Would madame care for a manicure?'

She wiped away a tear and nodded.

'A favourite style, perhaps? It is your birthday tomorrow, after all.'

She thought for a moment. 'Do ten different pictures.'

'Ten?' Dave paused. 'Then I shall tell you a story.'

He sat beside Sarah, flicked the loupe over one eye and set to work. His hands moved at fifty times normal speed, his fingers a blur, as though the pictures were being printed, rather than painted onto Sarah's nails.

As Dave painted the first nail, he began his story. 'A long time ago, a young girl lived in a house near the woods with her mother and father.' The first picture, on Sarah's left pinkie, showed a young girl running through a meadow, carrying wildflowers.

'One day, a genie came to their house, offering wealth and riches, so long as they let him stay in their house.' The second picture showed the genie: a powerful looking spirit who sat cross-legged, floating in the air.

'The family welcomed him into their home, and let him stay with them.' In the third picture, the family sat with the genie in front of the fire; their house filled with treasure. Goblets and other wares lay scattered across the floor.

'But the genie took more than he gave. When they were not looking, he stole their clothes, their food, and their memories.' A sinister, grimacing genie filled the fourth picture, hoarding food in his arms.

Dave dabbed brushes and needles into a palette which hovered beside him.

'One day, the man returned from working the fields to find the house empty, and the cupboards bare. The genie had taken the mother and the child, leaving him all alone.' In the fifth picture, the man knelt on the floor with his head in his hands. Tears streamed down his cheeks.

'The man left his home to search for the genie. He met with other travellers, all of whom had been deceived by the genie, and had lost that which they loved.' Travellers gathered round an inn table, sharing stories, in the sixth picture.

'Emboldened by their tales and by drink, the man hunted the genie through the woods.' An ancient forest in silhouette, lit by the light of the Milky Way, filled her seventh nail.

'Traps and danger awaited him at every turn, for the djinn was cunning. He slew dragons and giant spiders to reach the genie's lair.' A knight brandishing a flaming sword fought a red dragon in the eighth picture.

'The man outsmarted the genie: burning the forest, and trapping him in a small enclave.' Sarah's ninth nail showed the djinn consumed by flames, his face contorted in agony.

'As the genie burned, the man freed his wife and daughter, and they returned home to live the rest of their days in peace.' The final picture showed the family re-united in the meadow, the forest smouldering in the distance.

Sarah marvelled at the imagery. 'Wow, that's so coo—'

'—Ah, ah. It's not finished yet.' Dave inked stalks and stems in henna along Sarah's fingers, each tipped with a flower. They wound from her nails to her wrist, where their roots faded into skin.

'This story flows back to you, Sarah. You are the treasure and the riches. You are what your father fights for, each and every day.' Dave stepped away, his task complete.

'Awwww.' Sarah looked up to see Max watching her from the doorway.

She ran to her father, squeezed him as hard as she could and kissed his cheek. Max's heart soared as love flowed from his daughter once more. Sarah, it seemed, was back to normal.

Dave watched in silence, remembering that a fairy tale can bring a girl back to herself, and that love doesn't always shout. Sometimes, it's painted, one nail at a time.

***

Max stood in the living room, scotch in hand. A soft, late-night gloom hung in the air. He slouched against the wall beside Hockney's *Portrait of Nick Wilder*, a window into late-twentieth Californian glamour. In the painting, a man luxuriated in a swimming pool which glistened in the late afternoon sunshine. Low-rise apartments populated the background.

He stared at the painting for some time, leaning in, ever closer, as his mind drifted. As his head pierced the image, the picture hummed, snapping him from his reverie.

He poured another scotch.

'Ah, the edges of the simulation!' He turned and called to the house, 'Gotta watch that one, huh?' He staggered back to the sofa, and turned his attention to the video which played in the centre of the room. A screen showed footage of Sarah's school play from '64, where she had played the Big Bad Wolf.

'I'll huff and I'll puff and I'll blow your house down!' The video filled the room, transforming it into a stage. Cardboard cut-out trees lined the walls, while a spotlight shone on a wooden house centre stage.

'Play the party,' Max said.

Dave appeared at the doorway. 'We played it last wee—'

'—Play it.'

The video cut to footage of Sarah's fifth birthday. Dave entertained children in the back garden, as balloons and dragons filled the skies above. As the video cut to close-ups of Sarah, Max whispered along to the dialogue on-screen.

'Daddy, look!'

'What is it, love?'

'I got the dragon's tail.' Sarah held her plate aloft with pride.

'Careful. It makes you breathe fire!'

She pondered the thought for a moment, then said, 'I love you, Daddy.' She rubbed noses with her father in a clumsy *kunik*.

The video froze, then faded to black, and the lighting in the living room returned to its usual state.

He spotted Sarah standing at the doorway in her pyjamas, then paused, embarrassed. 'Hey. I… I didn't know you were still up.'

She saw tears in his eyes. 'Can't sleep. What's wrong?'

'Nothing, Love.' A pause. 'I miss you, that's all.' He tried to laugh it off.

'There's nothing to miss, Daddy. I'm right here.' She sat down and hugged Max.

After a moment, he asked, 'Love, what happened? We used to get along so well.'

She shrugged. 'I dunno. I just feel like you're always on my back.'

His voice was gentle, tender. 'I'm sorry I'm like this, I'm just… you're all I have left. If anything happened to you, I don't know what I'd do.'

'Daddy! Nothing's going to happen to me. Stop worrying so much.'

After a pause she spoke. 'I'm gonna stay at Mum's tomorrow night, okay?'

'But, your birthday. It's my turn this year. I thought we...' He opened his mouth, then closed it again. A pause. 'Okay, sure,' he sighed.

'Besides, you should go.' She tipped her head towards the card that sat on the coffee table.

'But how did you—?'

'—Dad, you should go. You need people. *I can't be your everything.* And… she's gorgeous.'

She kissed him on the cheek and made her way to bed.

His eyes landed on the card. He picked it up and spun it between his fingers.

*Divinity.*

***

He stood in the doorway, watching her sleep.

She curled beneath the blanket, head tucked into her chest like a fawn.

Her fringe had fallen across her brow. Max gently brushed it back, taking in the freckles scattered across her nose, the way she held the blanket fisted in one hand, the way her toes curled inward beneath the duvet like little commas.

'Jesus… twelve tomorrow,' he whispered.

He sat on the edge of the bed and watched her.

He had known how to love her as a child – with devotion, care, and patience. But as she grew, she needed his head as much as his heart. Love alone would not shepherd her through adolescence.

As a tween, she baffled him. He felt helpless, outpaced – and it would only get worse from here on in. She was outgrowing his emotional capacity, breaking free from his orbit, and venturing along her own trajectory.

His heart brimmed with love, yet doubt lingered.

He whispered, not to wake her, 'Six more years. How am I gonna cope?'

He turned, noticing Dave leaning against the landing wall. 'You should go,' Dave said, coolly.

Dave had read his mind. *Yes. I should go.*

He double-tapped the wall and the soft femto light receded, purples, blues and yellows fading to black as he closed the door.

# 6

# Midnight, the Stars and You

'Come on, then. Make me look good.' Max led Dave to the spare room. 'It's a noir theme, so I need to look the part.' He stood before a full-length mirror, twisting from side to side, eyeing his reflection.

Dave pulled up a large screen to one side. 'Well, there's a vintage Hollywood section.' A 5×4 grid of stars from Hollywood's golden age appeared on-screen, pouting and posing in pre-baked animation loops. They danced, smoked, tilted hats, and performed other idle animations. 'Would you like to preview skins with the filter?'

'Sure.' The colour faded from Max, and high contrast black and white rendered across his body, tracing the lines of his clothes and the architecture of his face. Soft focus made him appear warm and radiant.

He scrolled through the archive.

'Here. Cary Grant.' He tapped on the thumbnail to preview the skin. With his warm, delicate features, and iconic blue-grey plaid suit from *North By Northwest*, Grant was a paragon of grace, style, and old world glamour.

Dave tipped his head towards Max; a mark of respect. 'Well, well. He's a well-tailored one, isn't he?'

Max spoke in Grant's refined mid-Atlantic voice as he adjusted his tie. 'Well, you know what they say. The skin doesn't make the man. The man makes the skin.' He twisted to the side. 'I look good.'

'Yes, you do.' Dave straightened the collar and brushed a hair from Max's shoulder.

'Okay. Colourise. I'm gonna grab a drink.' The filter dissipated, and the skin colourised.

As Max filled his glass, Dave stepped closer. 'Perhaps just the one drink before you go out, Max? I've heard DeWinter's parties can get pretty wild.'

Sensing frustration, he softened his tone. 'It's okay, Max. She'll be okay. She's just gone to her Mum's for the night. That's all.'

The two men lingered in a stand-off for a moment, then Jeeves appeared at the door. 'Sir, your car has arrived.'

Max downed the whisky and made his way outside, as Dave warned, 'Be careful, Max.'

'Of what?'

Dave hesitated, for once unsure what to say.

'Just be careful.'

***

Outside, the car purred, its engine idling. The 1936 Duesenberg Model J was an icon of the Jazz Age, oozing old-world luxury: broad, bold, all Deco lines. The noir filter applied to the car, so while the world appeared in vivid, saturated hues, the car itself rendered in black and white. A spare tyre sat across the side panel beneath the steeply raked windscreen.

He spotted the number plate: MAX.

'Nice touch.'

As he climbed in, he entered the noir filter. The field filled the three-dimensional space, rendering the world – within and beyond the field – in high contrast black and white, with all the noise and imperfections of old celluloid. Soft focus lent the scene a warm, nostalgic feel.

The driver, in tie and suit, half-turned his head towards Max. 'Mr Fisher, is it, sir?' The old man was overly aestheticised and slightly artificial, as though modelled from a puppet, rather than a human.

'Yes.'

'Very good, sir. Jenkins, sir. I'll be your driver this evening.' He adjusted his position and drove off.

'Some music, sir?' Jenkins twisted a dial on the radio, passing through white noise before landing on a station playing upbeat swing.

They cruised through London in black and white, wartime jazz crackling through the hiss of an old FM tuner. London became stranger, alien – rendered as it would have appeared during the 1930s.

The drums pounded and the bass throbbed as they made their way across the river, towards the west, and to John DeWinter's famed home in Kensington Palace Gardens.

The car pulled up in front of the house. It was magnificent: an eighteenth century town home in the Regency style, built for London's ruling class, and big enough to contain a whole row of other houses. The sounds of conversation and old jazz filled the cavernous ballroom; so vast that a ghostly echo shimmered behind the main soundscape.

An elderly man with a cane approached Max as he entered the foyer. 'Ah, you must be the bookseller.'

'Yes, I must be.'

'Delighted to meet you, Max. John DeWinter.' He shook Max's hand, then bowed, raising his cane into the air. 'The host of this modest soirée.'

'A Night to Remember.' Max looked across the hall in awe.

'Let us hope so – and let us hope,' he whispered, 'for all the right reasons.' He was sharp, exuberant, boyish; with such poise that he seemed a much younger man. He had the air of a privileged life spent in theatre and the arts, rubbing shoulders with the rich and famous. His unpretentious dress – white linen trousers and black shirt – suggested a man entirely comfortable in his own skin.

Max gazed across the ballroom, where stars from the golden age mingled in tuxedos and cocktail dresses: Veronica Lake, Jean Marais, Louis Armstrong, Marlene

Dietrich, Coco Chanel, Lauren Bacall, Nat King Cole, and Billie Holiday.

'This is quite the party.'

'I should hope so, for the price.' DeWinter waved his cane towards various furnishings. 'I configured the décor using my collection,' he leaned in, raised his eyebrows and whispered, 'but these burlesque girls don't come cheap, you know.'

A large oil painting above the hearth caught Max's eye. Noticing his interest, DeWinter asked, 'Do you know the tale of *Apotheca's Feast of Merriment*?'

They approached the painting.

'Apotheca was a marquess, merchant, and patron of the arts who lived in southern England in the thirteenth century. His daughter, Miriam, was to be married to the Earl of Whitewood, who lived in the neighbouring county. To celebrate, Apotheca held a feast. Lords and ladies came from across the land, bringing with them gifts, and live oxen and calves for the slaughter.

'The feast took place one summer night at Apotheca's Hall in Sussex. These were prosperous, bountiful times – the dawn of international trade – which fostered a rare generosity of spirit among the nobility. The feast was celebrated in many a song and story – and here in this painting by Piero Marcovelli, from 1493.

'But forgive me – I forgot about our filter.' DeWinter called his wisp. 'Lucien? Colourise Marcovelli's diptych.'

The painting revealed its colours. Max surveyed the scene, which was indeed impressive. Lords and ladies came together, all banners under one roof, sharing food and wine, and celebrating Apotheca's wealth and prosperity. A pig roasted on a spit above the hearth. At one table, a lord handed a chicken leg to a dog. A jester played a fiddle in the corner, while a drunken baron danced with the servants.

'A tale of prosperity, compassion, and magnanimity. Now, come. Let me show you the second painting in this diptych, *Apotheca's Famine of Wanting*.'

DeWinter continued as he led Max down the hallway. 'Latterly, Apotheca's fortunes took a turn for the worse. With his daughter having left the family home to live with the Earl of Whitewood, Apotheca lost his sense of purpose. He grew lonely, despite his material comfort, with nothing but furnishings and servants to keep him company. He drank excessively, and would lash out at and beat his servants. One night, his ship, The Merry Siren, laden with riches from the East, and bound for England, sank in a storm just off the Cape of Good Hope. His fortune was lost.'

Max and DeWinter stood in front of *Apotheca's Famine of Wanting*.

'Apotheca invited the earls to his hall once more, hoping his famed generosity might be returned in kind. They came on one autumn day, but they too, had fallen on hard times. The season's harvest had failed, and King Henry III had levied taxes to defray the expense of the war with France. The cupboards were bare throughout the land. Apotheca asked his peers and his friends for food for the winter, but none could, or would, spare sustenance. He begged them, to no avail. In an act of desperation, Apotheca pulled a sword from above the hearth, and held it against the baron Henry Hussey's throat.

'The baron's guards drew their swords and lunged at Apotheca, but not before he had pierced Hussey's throat.'

Max took in the scene, which presented a heartbreaking inversion of the first painting. Breadcrumbs and leftovers were strewn across what had once been a lavish banquet table. Rats fought over scraps, and servants hid bread in their pockets.

Apotheca's body lay in a pool of blood, next to Baron Hussey's. The scene spoke of desperation and decline; of how the mighty fall when hard times befall them.

DeWinter spoke slowly as he reflected on the painting.

'Abundance becomes absence, the banquet turns to breadcrumbs, the dancing to bloodshed. The diptych is the story of every soul — of love found, then lost.'

His gaze lingered on the painting. 'When the sun shines on us, Mr Fisher, we are as angels. We are our brother's keeper: noble, magnanimous creatures; saints, no less. But when the sky darkens and the wind turns cold, we are as animals.

'Generosity, compassion, kindness: these values are circumstantial; contingent as they are upon material comfort. Without such comfort, we will tear each other apart.' His voice trailed off, as though he were reminiscing on painful memories.

'People are neither good nor bad, but fortune makes us so,' Max offered.

DeWinter smiled. 'Precisely, my boy.'

Max raised an eyebrow. 'I can see why you keep this one tucked away in the back.'

The old man laughed, placing a hand on Max's shoulder. 'Come, let us not dwell on suffering and loss. Let us drink. Paloma will perform soon.'

DeWinter clicked his fingers at a nearby Jeeves, who presented Max with a drink, and acknowledged him with a *sir*.

He led Max towards the ballroom. 'You're Divinity's friend, aren't you?'

'Yes, I suppose I am.'

'Such a charming young lady. Such fierce, free spirit. Such grace.' Max noticed that DeWinter found it difficult to walk. He hobbled, and wheezed a little. 'But, such is life: the good people of this world do not often meet with good fortune. Divinity has suffered hardship; hardship she has not deserved.' He stopped, turning to face Max. 'I can but hope that one day she finds happiness.

'And what about you? What is it you seek? Why did you come here tonight?'

'I… I'm not sure.'

'There is much to see and much to learn, Max. Come see me after Paloma's concert. Upstairs, in my office.' He smiled as he concluded, 'Now, come. The night is young, and who knows what pleasures await you this fine evening? Go find Divinity. She's in there somewhere.' He motioned Max inside.

As Max turned to bid DeWinter farewell, he was already greeting his next guest, his arms spread wide.

'Clarissa, my dear! The hall brightens.'

***

The noir filter rendered across the property, lending the scene a lavish, filmic quality. The effect was breathtaking, like living in an old movie. Decolourisation brought out shapes, forms, and shadows brilliantly. Guests moved like ghosts of the silver screen — exuberant, timeless. The world was starker, sadder, colder in black and white, but it made for one hell of a party.

A bar stretched the length of the ballroom. On the wall opposite, a projector cast *The Third Man* across a vast screen. Trapeze artists and tightrope walkers soared above the dance floor, while Jeeves bots passed among the crowd holding trays laden with champagne and canapés. Holographic bands played early twentieth jazz on a stage to the rear. Ray Noble and His Orchestra rendered as translucent, crackling holograms, playing their haunting tune, *Midnight, The Stars And You*. Models, actors, and singers arced across the dance floor in sync with the music. It was part ballroom, part circus: a theatre of the rich and famous, through the lens of classical Hollywood.

The tune faded out and the orchestra glitched into an African-American band playing lindy hop and jitterbug. They worked the crowd hard through tempo changes, modulations, and solos. Dancers spun and swung each other round, cheered on by the crowd. They moved fast, almost faster than the music, like how old films would look sped up, as if life itself moved faster back then.

The crowd was a mix of chiselled American glamour and European decadence. Some wore Venetian masks, while others wore body art across one side of their face; some providing a flourish on the cheek, others around the eyes.

A woman walked past Max with a large picture frame hung around her head, as though she herself were a work of art. Her head rendered in a Cubist style, as though her face had been broken into pieces and then reassembled, like something Picasso might have painted.

A man wearing a monocle and top and tails stood to one side of the dance floor, drinking absinthe. An owl perched on his shoulder, watching the room.

A woman, clearly drunk, laughed at her own reflection in a mirror to one side of the hall. She laughed so hard that tears ran down her face, spoiling her makeup.

The effect was intoxicating – and most of the guests were already drunk. It was hard to tell where the simulation ended and reality began. Couples paired up on the dance floor, lost in ecstasy. People smoked cigarettes that weren't real, and drank rum and gin that were. Smoke lingered in the air above the dance floor, limp and harmless. It was indeed a night to remember.

A voluptuous woman who reminded Max of a young Sophia Loren approached, wearing a snake around her neck.

'Well, hello, beautiful,' she slurred. The snake reared its head at Max, hissing. The woman cackled as Max startled and walked away.

'How the hell am I gonna find her? And how's she gonna find me?' he muttered.

As he scanned the crowd, another woman approached from behind and placed a hand on his shoulder. She spoke with an American accent.

'Far out, huh?'

He looked her up and down. 'I'll say.'

She was a flapper: a cultural icon, the embodiment of the liberated woman of the 1920s and '30s. She wore a sequinned dress, nude stockings with a floral print, a pearl necklace, and – it seemed – very little else. Her short, cropped bob signalled a break from the past: a middle finger to Victorian norms. Powder and rouge lent contrast and definition to her features.

It was pure deco: the body as art.

She was dazzling.

'You looking for someone?' she asked.

'Yes, a friend.'

The woman raised the palm of her hand in front of her face, freezing her image in place, as another face peered out from behind the render. It was Divinity, in colour. Her smile lit the room.

She winked at Max, then whispered in her real voice. 'Me too.'

She retreated again behind her mask and lowered her hand, and once again the flapper stood before Max. In hindsight, he could just about recognise her in the skin. Her face and features were more rounded, her hips more curvaceous, but her eyes betrayed her. She placed a hand on her hip, and tipped her head towards Max. 'How do I look?'

'Divine. But how did you know—'

She placed a forefinger on his lips. 'Come on, Cary.' She threaded her arm through his and led him to the bar. 'Buy me a drink.'

They sipped whisky sours and watched the dance floor. Divinity turned to Max. 'Wasn't sure you'd come.'

'How could I say no? This is quite the party, and you're quite the date.'

'Well, Paloma's got a new book out, and John can never say no to a party.'

'What's the book about?'

'Noir thriller. Something about love and death in Paris.'

She looked across the ballroom and sighed. 'Can you believe it's come to this? The carnival of the unreal. A simulation on top of a simulation.'

'Hey, you invited me. It's not my party.'

'I'm serious, Max. Look at this place. It's the fucking simulacrum.'

'The what?'

'The point where image replaces reality.' She quoted from Eden's promotional materials, *'More real than the real thing,* right? We're aching for meaning in a world that numbs. Trapped in a labyrinth, with no way out. We don't even know what real means any more.' She took another sip from her drink.

'Yeah. Sometimes it all just feels like a dream.'

'It is. It's a circus. A hall of mirrors, designed to hide the truth.'

'What truth?'

'That this world is more broken than it looks.'

She glanced away, then spoke again – slower. 'Don't you ever want to look beyond the veil?'

'Every day.' He winced, knowing he was just trying to please her.

She smiled and took his hand.

'Come on, Cary. Let's dance.'


The lights dimmed, leaving the room in darkness, save for an area of the dance floor where shone a lone spotlight. The crowd went quiet, as all eyes turned to the solitary figure in the middle of the room.

Paloma Carhartt – singer, writer, society girl – stood in the limelight, her body outstretched and poised, arms held high. She'd risen to fame in London's party scene of the '60s, and had established herself as a writer with her 2066 debut, *Upon A Moon And A Star*, the story of a teacher's affair with a student in mid-twentieth Algiers. Four years later, she was preparing to publish her follow-up, *A Night to Remember*.

She held her pose, teasing the crowd, radiant in stillness. A white lace dress draped from her shoulders, sequins and crystals catching the light. A champagne headdress with pearls and ostrich feathers crowned the deco queen.

The drums began. Spotlights flared on two sailors who spun her across the floor, clarinets climbing higher and higher.

The sailors tossed her wide – she froze mid-spin, arms outstretched, blew a kiss into the dark.

The song modulated upward, building to climax. The sailors launched her into a reverse somersault. As she landed in their arms – arms spread wide – the song ended, and the audience erupted.

The crowd settled as she took the mic on stage.

She spoke to the band, then turned to the crowd. 'Ladies and gentlemen, mesdames et messieurs, boys and girls; literati, glitterati, inebriati. Tonight, let us make love in London. Let us be free, let us wander, let our spirits soar, in honour of John and this fine soirée.' Cheers echoed across the dance floor and glasses clinked. 'I would like to sing this next song for my darling John.' She blew a kiss into the crowd, sparking whoops and hollers.

The pianist played a lazy ballad; ghostly musical notes drifting from his Steinway. The dance floor filled with couples and romance blossomed as Paloma sang of love and longing.

> *I'm dreaming you near, though I know you're far,*
> *Pretending your heart is still mine.*
> *I sway through the dark with shadow for grace,*
> *A whisper that once was a kiss.*

DeWinter glided in from stage right, joining Paloma. The crowd roared, elated to see the legendary actor on-stage again. He sang the male part, repeating the verse alongside Paloma.

It made for a surreal, dream-like experience. It seemed for a time as though a fish eye lens distorted the world, bringing the stage closer and wrapping Max in Paloma's spell.

DeWinter danced with Paloma during the piano solo, before singing the finale together, to rapturous applause.

He bowed and left the stage, and silence descended on the room. Paloma picked up a conductor's baton from one side of the stage, and caressed the rod in her hands, clearly tipsy. 'You know, a lot of people have asked me how I wrote *Upon A Moon And A Star*. Let me show you.'

She whispered a few words to the musicians, raised her baton, and conducted the band in a lively ragtime number, whipping the crowd into a frenzy. Characters blurred into each other, and it became hard to tell which face belonged to whom. Actors and models danced on tables with abandon. The air was hot, sticky. It was pure spectacle, the dawn of the modern age.

Divinity leaned in to Max. 'Come on, handsome.'

She led him to the bar, past strange women with cats and snakes, and past the woman who came as a painting.

She signalled to the bartender, then turned to Max. 'Tell me about your daughter.'

'She's everything. Brilliant, stubborn. Funny without trying.'

Divinity studied his face. 'You love her madly.'

'More than she knows.' He paused, then asked, 'Why'd you reach out to me?'

She looked into her glass. 'Because I know what it means to lose someone.'

He nodded. 'I'm sorry. That's not easy.'

'No, it's not,' she sipped her drink, 'but it teaches you how to listen.'

A quiet passed between them.

'So,' he asked gently, 'why me?'

She met his gaze. 'Because I saw something in you.'

'Saw…?'

She leaned in, her voice low. 'Can you trust me, Max?'

He raised an eyebrow. 'I don't know. Can I?'

She tilted her head, and her expression changed.

She sniffed the air, frowning. 'Can you smell smoke?'

An ageing man pushed through the crowd in full colour. He ogled partygoers, seemingly drunk or high. His long hair streaked silver and violet.

Guests edged away, repulsed by the artless figure, who flickered and glitched, as though a DJ were scratching holographic video. He grabbed a Katherine Hepburn on the dance floor and kissed her.

'Divinity!'

'Come on.' Divinity led Max through the crowd. Behind Jak, Katherine Hepburn wiped her mouth, aghast.

'I know that guy,' Max said. 'He was looking for you.'

'Yeah, he does that.'

Jak's voice boomed with echo and reverb. 'Still running, Rahmani?'

He ate another grape, flicked his cigarette into a champagne glass, then cracked his whip across an emptying dance floor.

Lightning split the room, and a storm raged in the hall.

The band glitched, before fading into silence.

Jak's rain spread, colourising revellers and furnishings and leaving unnerving, broken renders. Guests stumbled as their faces melted, eyes and mouths slipping like paint.

Doors and windows dissolved into blank walls. Snakes hissed across the floor.

Divinity pulled Max. 'John. We need to reset the field.'

Jak's body flickered, seams of static running up his arms. Shadows bled from his frame, warping the light around him.

Another whip-crack. Jak's scarred face stretched across the walls, tiled across every surface.

As Divinity and Max approached the foyer, a scream pierced the air. An old man lay on the floor, in colour, his throat slit.

'John!' Divinity fell to her knees beside him.

After a breath, she stood and turned to a nearby Jeeves. 'Where's your intercom?'

'This way, Ma'am.' He led them to an alcove, where she spotted the unit.

Rain fell on the intercom, melting colour and monochrome together – but it still worked. Divinity pulled the keyboard from the machine, and keyed in a few lines of code.

```
C:\DEWIN\fieldcommand int reset
C:\DEWIN\wispren reset
C:\DEWIN\wispconfig /renew
OK: wispconfig renew; round trip time 3ms
```

The world around them flickered, then settled.

She approached from behind, knife in hand, eyes locked on Jak and Meph. The wisp controlled the audiovisual field, so if either of them saw her coming, she was toast.

Meph spun, eye wide. Clocked, Divinity turned on her heel and bolted for cover.

Jak cracked his whip. It snaked round her ankle and yanked her down. She cried out as he reeled her in, the slack tightening, hooks biting deeper into her flesh the more she resisted. She clawed at the carpet, slashing at the whip with her knife – in vain.

Max charged from the other side and smashed a vase across Jak's face. Jak hit the floor, his head bouncing off hardwood. The whip slackened.

As Jak groaned, Max seized Meph.

Divinity lay on the ground, breath heaving, praying the final line of code had executed:

```
C:\DEWIN\disable local wispdef
```

She writhed, waiting for pain – for electricity, rupture – but none came. Max crushed the droid underfoot before it could reboot. Sparks crackled as its lights flickered and faded to black.

Jak sprawled on the floor: bleeding, broken, his assault failing.

As Meph's compute functions failed, the ballroom shimmered – noise, glitches, chaos peeling away – until the scene rendered once more in elegant noir.

Max crouched and struck Jak in the face. 'Relax, man. You had a bad fall.' He punched the same spot the vase had cut, flattening him. 'That's it.' Another punch. 'Take it easy.'

He helped Divinity free herself, and they scrambled towards the exit.

As they walked away, Jak propped himself on one elbow, wiping blood from his nose. 'I'll find you, pretty boy.'

Divinity pulled Max towards the exit, her pulse racing. 'How the hell did you catch that thing?'

'Right place, right time, I guess.'

'That guy… That's what I mean. This world, it hollows people.'

'Not you.'

She smiled, 'Come on. Let's go.'

He led her to the Duesenberg, where Jenkins waited. 'Sir, ma'am. I trust you had a pleasant evening?'

'Unforgettable. Take us home, Jenkins.'

'Very well, sir.'

***

The car threaded through the city, following the contour of the Thames through Pimlico and Westminster. The cityscape appeared mostly in silhouette; dark, brooding towers stretching high into the sky. The world outside ebbed and flowed in soft focus, the background seemingly on a loop, as the radio played an old wartime song. The Duesenberg's straight-eight engine purred beneath the lullaby.



Divinity stared out the window, slack and distant. 'I like this song. It's honest. Dream your cares away, forget about your problems. Anything to escape the void.'

'You're not a dream. You're real. Aren't you?' He elicited a smile. 'I'm sorry about John.'

'He used to say, never let your guard down. You gotta grow eyes in the back of your head. Guess he finally slipped up.' She sighed in frustration and punched the side of the car. 'God damn it.

'This world can ruin you, Max. Fall too deep, and you won't know what's real any more.' She looked ahead, into the distance. 'I've seen people disappear down the rabbit hole.'

'This guy, Jak. He got in too deep. The drugs degraded his body, he couldn't sleep – and the worse he got, the more crazy shit he did.'

She turned away, trying to collect her thoughts. 'This place, it's a drug. It calls you when you're low, takes away our inner peace.'

'Back at the party, John was gonna help me. With what?'

'This place… it's stardust, Max. It slips through your fingers.'

A glow stirred in the sky as they crossed Westminster Bridge. A starfield time-lapse bloomed, trailing the light of a thousand stars.

She smiled, wistful. 'One last flourish from John.' A tear streamed from her eye.

He leaned in and spoke softly. 'The starlight slows to linger in your presence.'

The moment hung, suspended in light, disarming Divinity.

'You've got to admit, it's beautiful,' he whispered.

She wiped away the tear. 'Yeah. Eden has its moments.'

'So do you.'

'You're sweet,' she smiled, placing a hand on his cheek, as her eyes softened, 'pretty boy.'

They kissed in black and white to the sounds of wartime jazz and ghostly classical. Her perfume laced the air with spices, vetiver, and yuzu. The carnival of light reached its finale, as the starfield dissipated and glitter rained across the city.

***

They stepped out of the car into the soft-lit wash of default reality. The world denoired, and the cinematic haze dissolved.

He swiped the Cary Grant skin away, fading into Home Three.

'Well, hello Max.' She was even more beautiful in colour.

He bowed, beckoning her inside. 'Madam.'

Dave called from the living room as they entered. 'Evening. How was the part—?'

He paused in the hallway, spotting Divinity.

'Sorry – didn't realise you had company.' He looked away, flustered. 'I was just heading to bed. Breakfast at eight?'

'Nine,' Max replied.

Divinity tried to suppress laughter as Dave left. 'Nice to meet you, Dave.'

They stood mere inches apart in Max's bedroom, which rendered as the scene from Rousseau's *The Snake Charmer*. The walls fell away, revealing a painterly jungle scene.

Vines and palms cloaked the rainforest. The sound of cicadas and birdsong hung in the air. Creatures foraged nearby, rustling the undergrowth, as the full moon bathed the riverbank in soft light. Ripples shimmered across flowing water.

The scene was lit in an impressionistic style. It was that hour between night and morning, when magic still breathes. Pastel greens and soft blues washed over the sky and the river.

She took his hands in hers, and let out a sigh. 'My, my. You do have good taste.'

He stepped closer, his eyes locked on hers.

'Yes, I do.'

A pink spoonbill emerged from the water and waddled up the bank.

'Depth of field,' Max whispered to the room, blurring the background, and leaving himself and Divinity in sharp focus.

They embraced under the moon on the banks of the faraway river. Folk music played in the distance – a flute, or *bansuri*, perhaps.

The night was warm, her body warmer still.

# 7

# Your Dreams Belong To Us

He woke early. Mouth dry. Head sore.

He stared at empty walls – the room's default configuration. Rousseau's brushstrokes and blue-green light were gone. But for the woman beside him, it might've been any other Sunday.

She sprawled, one foot dangling. Jak's whip had torn her leg, deep welts blooming across her shin.

He clambered out of bed and pulled on his boxers. 'Damn it, why do I open on Sundays?'

He spotted Dave leaning against the doorway, arms folded. The construct spoke softly. 'You're leaving her here?'

'Let her rest. Rough night.' He looked again at the cuts on Divinity's leg. 'Give her some breakfast, will you?'

'Certainly. Jeeves will tend to her wounds when she wakes up. She'll be back on her feet in no time.'

Max called back as he headed downstairs. 'And Sarah's back later. Tidy up, get him to cook something, okay?'

***

Willow drifted in lazy orbits around Max as they crossed the park.

'Who is *she*?' Her voice was curious, sing-song.

'Not now.'

'She looked important. Important to you.'

'Not now, Willow.'

'But I need to know—'

He swiped across her, zipping her mouth shut. She glared at him in mock fury.

At the train station, footage played on giant screens promoting The Day of the Night. Supernatural skins rotated on a carousel, as a host listed offers and promotions.

The footage cut to The Skeleton King: a titanic creature leading the parade through Piccadilly and Soho towards St Paul's. He towered above the city, taller than any building, wearing a brown fur cloak and golden crown, and holding a jewelled bone staff.

Max found a quiet spot on the train. Willow settled beside him, lenses fluttering.

'Snooze.'

She unzipped her mouth. 'Rest, sir. I shall hush the world.'

She dimmed the world – brightness and volume fading to 20%. The world fell silent and tinted sepia, its tones drifting softer to quiet the senses.

He closed his eyes and thought of Divinity.


A sudden metal clang jolted him awake.

Howls echoed from the platform as the train pulled into Kennington.

The doors slid open.

Another crash. Something hammering the carriage from outside.

A woman called out, 'Hello? Pretty boy?' – her voice sweet, uncanny. Kisses crackled through the air.

Movement on the platform – four, maybe five figures, blurred and indistinct.

'Mute local.'

The soundscape failed to reconfigure.

'I'm sorry. I can't,' Willow replied.

'Again. Mute local.'

'Something's pressing on me. The node… I can't hush it.'

The gang boarded through the adjacent carriage. Their steps made no sound. The world dimmed a fraction, as though lighting cues had shifted. Two of them stepped aside. Between them – glitching gently, barely contained – stood a figure Max recognised.

A voice arrived before the man did – slow, submerged, as though remembered from a dream.

'You were dreaming of me, weren't you?'

The face assembled in fragments – grin first, then eyes.

Reality pulsed.

Jak's body flickered between skins: cowboy, priest, hangman, lover. None quite held. His fur coat trailed glitches. His sunglasses – heart-shaped and perched low on his nose – played a silent collage of old MTV videos, each lens split into a grid of pop fragments. His hair shifted through the colour spectrum at the tips.

He peered over the sunglasses, eyes gleaming with some private joke.

Behind him: a gang of four, led by xXCaTRiNaXx, Queen of Death.

She was an imposing vision of *La Catrina* – carnival queen, white and skeletal. Her red-and-black dress shimmered as she floated inches above the floor. Roses crowned her skull. The songs of sirens emanated from her – not music, but lure.

The others gathered behind her like avatars from lost mythologies – a *Yakuza* gangster with tattoo-spiders crawling across his face, a Nigerian punk in scorched denim who trailed lava, an unholy priest with four faces from ancient theatre.

The two sides froze in a stand-off.

Max leapt from his seat and bolted toward the next carriage. He stumbled, disoriented, as the carriage warped.

Jak ran a visual subroutine. Reality creaked. The walls pulsed. The exit vanished beneath fake panelling.

Max swiped the air, found the handle, and staggered into the next carriage.

The world changed again.

Purple velvet walls, floating balloons, and a dreamy waltz from a cracked organ. Painted dolls and jester-heads sprang from the walls. The world tilted, throwing him off-balance. He tripped and fell. Snakes rippled across the floor, snapping.

He stumbled into the next carriage – a black expanse. Galaxies and nebulae shimmered in the distance – Fox Fur, Medusa, the Ghost of Jupiter.

He fell, hitting his head on the edge of a seat.

The simulation blinked, and the train snapped back into place.

He wiped blood from his brow as the gang closed in.

Meph's tractor beam caught Willow. The pixie shrieked as she was suspended in a pulsating sphere.

Jak's DJ shader scratched, his face warping in sync with the stutter it masked.

He crouched and grabbed Max by the throat. 'Where is she?'

Max stared, still dazed. 'What?'

Jak glitched, his words rewound in a DJ spinback.

'Rahmani. Where is she?' He tightened his grip.

'I don't know. She left.'

Jak leaned in, nose brushing Max's neck.

'Don't lie to me. I can smell her on you. She echoes in your code.'

He struck. Max doubled over.

The punk rocker stepped forward. A vocoder effect lent his speech a metallic, glossy sheen. 'A martyr, huh?'

Jak turned. Then pivoted back, driving a boot into Max's gut.

'You think she'd come back for you?' Jak murmured. 'She's gone, Fisher – like your daughter.'

The gang stirred.

Jak crouched again, closer now.

'Won't talk?' A sigh. 'Then I guess I'll have to unzip you.'

He drew the knife, gems sparkling on its hilt.

Max kicked him, hard. Jak hit the floor, *Freyr* sliding out of reach.

Max pounced, landing two punches before Jak reversed him and slammed a fist into his jaw, then dragged him upright by the collar.

'Talk – or your daughter doesn't make it home.'

Max spun, reversed their positions, and pinned Jak against the carriage wall.

Jak's face reddened, and he began to fade.

With *Freyr* out of reach, he drew his electroshock stick, *Tempest*.

The weapon crackled and fizzed as it charged.

'Welcome to the real world, pretty boy.' He jammed the stick into the nerve cluster in Max's neck.

Max's body lit up, twitching.

He dropped, bile rising.

xXCaTRiNaXx heard sirens in the distance. 'Drones.' The train held at Waterloo, a cluster of droids scanning it.

'Jak, incoming!'

Jak crouched next to Max and spoke softly, placing a hand on Max's head. 'I'll find her, pretty boy. Don't worry. I'll find her. Your daughter, too.'

He turned to the gang. 'De-render.'

As his assailants faded into nothingness, so did Max. He watched them vanish into thin air, then passed out, bile dripping from his mouth and blood trickling down his neck.

***

'Sir, can you hear me? Sir?'

He drifted in dreamspace.

'Sir, can you hear me? Sir?' A maternal, calm voice. He opened his eyes, blinded by the afternoon light.

Through haze, a female figure in white – radiant, indistinct.

As his vision normalised, he recognised Devi, skinned as Saraswati. Her hummingbird, Gutna, hovered nearby.

Devi's render crackled like analogue TV, flickering in and out; her connection faltering.

'Sir… ca… hear me?' She clicked her fingers in front of his face, trying to rouse him.

He whispered, his voice hoarse, crackling. 'Devi. What happened?'

'Sir, your hardware has been damaged.'

She traced a screen in the air, conjuring a display, and scrolled through files.

'No hack attempts detected.' She flickered. 'The software's intact, but the hardware… Boy.'

He propped himself up. Pain coursed through him. He clutched his forehead. 'God, my head!'

She placed a virtual hand on his cheek. 'You must rest, sir. No sudden movements.'

'How long was I out for?'

'Around three hours, sir. Let's get you home. We need to reboot your system.'

He panicked, remembering Jak's words. 'Sarah. Where's Sarah?'

'She returned from her mother's this morning. She is safe and well.'

'Okay. Take me home, Dev.' He lifted himself from the floor and saw that the carriage was packed with passengers who stared at him in silence.

He looked out of the window to get his bearings. The train was heading south across the Thames. He must have drifted up and down the line for hours.

As he looked across the carriage, his visuals began to glitch. For a moment, the scene rendered as a black-and-white wireframe. The environment darkened. Passengers and architecture flickered into outline. Surfaces appeared as colourless, untextured polygons, as though the life had been drained from the world.

A moment later, the world re-rendered – darker, stranger, washed-out, like old film stock. The passengers appeared as simple, uniform figures, as if copy-pasted across the carriage. They wore white, rubbery bodysuits: skintight, featureless. Hair and clothing were gone; only holes for eyes, nose, and mouth hinted at the human beneath.

Stains daubed the carriage; cracks ran through the ceiling. Graffiti scarred the windows. A screech filled the carriage, as if the train grated on rusted tracks.

The scene flickered then reset. The cracks disappeared, the colours and soundscape normalised, and the train was once filled with regular passengers, who returned to their conversations.

He collapsed into a nearby seat, rubbed his eyes, trying to clear his head. His hands were shaking. He folded his arms, resting his head against the window.

As the train passed London Bridge into Southwark, the world around him glitched again. Textures and objects flickered, desaturated, and seemed to lose their post-processing effects.

Animated graffiti blinked out, revealing ghost artwork beneath the simulation. On cracked brick walls, Max made out all caps slogans and signoffs from another world:

SUBSCRIBE TO LIFE
WHAT DOES IT ALL MEAN?
YOUR DREAMS BELONG TO US

They were simple, crude scrawls, redolent of old aerosol sprays. The graffiti flickered as white noise and system glitches tried to erase it.

The world flickered and returned to its default configuration. The giant sequoias of the Great Forest towered once more above the city, and the train again filled with beautiful, happy people.

Max stared out of the window, desperate to get home.

The last slogan lingered, burned into his mind:

YOUR DREAMS BELONG TO US.

# 8

# The Conversation

'I'll take it from here, Devi.' Dave met them at the front door, glitching like a badly tuned TV.

Devi, Great Goddess, Mahadevi, Mother of the Universe, bowed and pressed her palms together in *añjali mudrā* before drifting away, leaving Max in Bowie's care.

Willow's circuits were cooked. Her flight functions shot, she crawled inside, groaning.

Max held a hand against his neck to stem the bleeding and steady the glitching.

'Where's Sarah?' he asked, breathless.

'Upstairs. In her room,' Dave replied.

Max scrambled up the stairs. 'Love, I'm home.'

'Hey!' Sarah called back through the walls.

He slipped into the bathroom. The room glowed with premium textures. Amber femto light softened the lightscape. A burner laced the room with ambrette, myrrh, and patchouli.

Something felt off. Too perfect. Too staged.

The textures crackled and fizzed. The bath flickered to a generic white. Shelves blinked to emptiness – just a toothbrush and a glass – before resetting.

For a moment, Max thought he might throw up.

He'd left the door ajar. 'You have fun at your mum's?' he called, dabbing blood from his brow.

'Yeah, good, thanks.'

'That's great, love. That's great.'

He locked the door, faced the mirror, turned on the tap. Blood traced his collarbone. The wound looked modest but burned like hell. The electroshock's teeth had gouged the flesh and torn at a nerve. He soaked the towel and pressed it to the cut.

Dave hovered behind him in the mirror. 'Your hardware's corrupted, Max. Hard reset required. Lie down. Jeeves and I will take care of it.'

Max ignored him and traced the wound with his fingers. Beneath the skin: a hard bump, jagged, metallic. A device of some kind, lodged inside him.

Knocking rattled the door. 'Daddy! I need the loo. Hurry up!'

'Give me a minute, love.' His eyes stayed on the wound.

'Max, don't touch it,' Dave warned. 'Jeeves is a capable anaesthetist. Let us help.'

Static flared. Max's face in the mirror warped, pixels crawling across it. A stranger looked back: bleached hair, stubble, eyes bright. Kid Riley, lead singer of The Burning Bees. His lips moved in time with Max's.

Max spoke, but Riley's husky drawl slipped out. 'What the hell...?'

Dave cut in. 'The software's corrupted. It's reaching into your archives. Lie down, Max. We can fix it.'

Max called to the house, 'Emergency BIOS. Mother, hard reset visuals.' His render crackled and warped momentarily, then snapped back to Kid Riley.

'Hard reset visuals,' he repeated.

A female voice answered from everywhere and nowhere, 'Access denied.'

'Override. Security code Seven Four Ampersand Charlie Mike Romeo Tango.'

'Access denied. Hardware error. User unauthorised. Please rest.' Mother's voice warped and fractured.

His face glitched again and another figure bloomed in the mirror: an old Sadhu, blue-faced, wrapped in an orange *angarkha*, jewellery rattling as he moved. The holy man's eyes were hollowed out.

Sarah hammered on the door. 'Daddy, I'm serious! Let me in or I'm gonna wet myself.'

'Just a sec, love,' Max called, unsure whose voice she heard.

He grabbed tweezers from the shelf, hands trembling. Flashing lights emerged from the ceiling, casting the room in red light and blasting a siren.

'Warning,' Dave snapped. 'Do not interfere with implants. You'll destabilise your system.'

'Override.' The skin was loose around the wound, almost hanging off. He drove the tweezers in.

'Max,' said Dave, 'don't touch it.'

'Bugger off, Dave. It fucking hurts.'

His reflection glitched again – himself, with his hair broken into jagged lines of code.

'Okay,' he muttered. 'Me again.'

Something caught on the tweezers. He pulled – a white film, taut, elastic, clinging like a second skin. The film crackled, as though software were trying to erase it.

'Max put the tweezers down,' Dave warned.

Sarah's fists hammered on the door. 'Daddy! Come on, it's not fair! I'm dying here.'

'Just a second, love.' He pulled the film harder, a small piece of metal emerging from inside the wound: some kind of diode, with two prongs at one end. He gripped and yanked. Pain spiked, as though a needle were being extracted from his body.

'Got it.' As he held the device, an LED light faded and the diode emitted a short fizzing noise, as though powering down.

# ANALOGUE

The world disintegrated into a new render, the air shifting as though his ears had repressurised after a flight. Dave was absent, and the banging on the door stopped.

The house was silent.

A strange image rendered in the mirror, which now appeared grubby and stained. A white membrane covered his body – thin, skintight, like a wetsuit – the same worn by the passengers on the train. The suit had openings for the eyes, nose, mouth, and – he would later discover – other orifices.

Time stalled as he studied the ghost in the mirror. He tilted his head, watching himself through eyes without a face; the reflection mirroring his movements.

'What the fuck?' he whispered, stroking his face. The membrane dulled his senses, like rubber gloves, and made it difficult to discern texture, pressure, or temperature.

He began tearing the membrane from his body. A cut in the fabric around the wound provided a starting point. He peeled it from his face in slow spirals. The film flaked from his nose, eyes, and cheeks, revealing the face beneath a lifetime of renders.

Though he recognised the face, it did not seem his own. Broad features, deep-set eyes, square jaw – but ten years older, and ten years worse. His skin was dull, pasty, lacking in vitality. His neck sagged. He leaned in and pulled down the skin beneath one eye. His eyes seemed his own – deep set and blue – though duller and less brilliant than he remembered them, and bloodshot.

He opened his mouth to look inside – poking and prodding his jaw, squeezing one cheek between his fingers.

He pierced the membrane around his wrists with the tweezers, freeing his hands, then peeled away the film from his neck and shoulders.

Beneath the membrane, his body was covered in a translucent mucus. His hair was oily, short, and messy; squashed by the membrane.

He recoiled at his face in the mirror. He was pale, undernourished, his hair thin and patchy. He looked like the ghost he had feared he might become.

His eyes scanned the bathroom, which was now marked by simple features and utilitarian design. The bath, sink, toilet, and shower appeared in white porcelain – default textures, stained and pitted. Black mould lined the corners.

Toiletries lay on cracked paint shelves – plain, unanimated. At the far end of the bath, the bonsai tree beneath which Dr Anderson slept was nowhere to be seen. In its place, an old soap dish.

The colour was different in this new world: washed out, dull, lifeless. Gone were the post-processing and the femto light which made the world pop and sparkle. Object animations were disabled, leaving the room unnervingly quiet.

The air was hot and sticky. Outside, a vicious wind battered the house.

His heart sank.

This was the analogue world: the space beneath the render.

This was a quieter, duller world.

This was the real world.

***

A house grows much like a garden. Over time, life takes root in its walls, on bookshelves, and in dusty corners.

He crept along the landing, the air thick with dust and decay. Shabby bookcases lined the walls, their shelves topped with photos. The spare room stood empty but for a single mirror in the corner – the one he had used to dress for the party. A diagonal fracture split the glass.

The house seemed hollow, a limp echo of itself. Plaster cracked along the walls.

'Sarah?' He crept towards her room.

'Sarah?' The door creaked open, the air musty. Toys and clothes from a much younger child hung from the rack. A rocking horse wore a unicorn tiara. Ted-E and Donk-E slumped on a shelf above the bed, their stuffing protruding. One of the bear's eyes dangled by a thread.

A pang spiked in his neck – the ghost of the torn diode. He heard it crackle, as though the simulation whispered one last time.

Somewhere in the walls, faint at first, came the clack… clack… clack of porcelain teeth. Max froze.

*M'ia o' the Candlelyte*'s cracked, lilting tones echoed from the hush between the inside and outside:

*T'ruth in its bones, ache in its breth,*
*It suckle silence, it rattle death.*
*A tale be told that ne'er was true,*
*The mask be worn, but not by you.*

A final whisper, barely a breath:

*The thread pulls yonder.*

The clacking stirred, then ebbed into nothing as the walls fell silent.

Downstairs, the air was dark and dank. On a plate beside the sink lay a dark paste, insect legs protruding.

The lights flickered before dying. A mug lay on the table, stained, chipped on the inner rim, and with a hairline crack running through the text 'World's Best Dad'.

A whirring mechanical sound came from the living room. 'Jeeves?'

Jeeves sat on the sofa, twitching in a loop – head turning, mouth opening to speak, snapping back, and starting again.

Max crouched beside the droid. 'Jeeves. Can you hear me?'

The droid startled and broke out of his loop for a moment. He looked Max up and down and sighed, 'Oh.'

'Jeeves, what's going on? Where's Sarah?'

The droid struggled to speak. 'Sir, please await further i-i-i-i-iiiiii-instructions.' His voice slowed down and spec up as he spoke. 'Central has been informed of this incident, and will d-d-d-d-dispatch units presently.'

'Jeeves, talk to me. What's happening?' Max tapped the droid's cheek, trying to bring him back.

The bot placed a hand on Max's and looked him in the eye, clearly struggling and in pain.

'G-g-g-good luck, s-s-sir.'

A gurgling sound escaped him. He lowered his head, chin resting on his chest, eyes closing for the last time.

'Max? Max, can you hear me?' A voice came from afar; refined, gentle. 'Over here, Max.'

'Dave?' he called to the house, unsure where to turn to.

'The intercom, Max.'

The intercom. *Of course.*

Dave appeared on the nanocell screen in his *Aladdin Sane* skin: a fragile mannequin split by a red-and-blue lightning bolt across his face. A metallic droplet clung to his collarbone, occasionally dripping.

'Dave. What the hell?'

The construct's voice garbled, phased. 'I'm sorry to see you like this, Max. I tried to help you. I really did.'

'What's happening?'

'You extracted your connection node. Your somatosensory interface.'

Max stared blankly.

'Your interface, Max. You're offline. The thugs on the train damaged it. Jeeves and I could have fixed you, if you'd lain down.'

Max tugged at the loose membrane hanging from his shoulders. 'What is this?'

'Your skin. A nanographene exosuit. It replicates touch, pressure, warmth – the feeling of holding a loved one, a summer breeze, the warmth of a fire. What it cannot emulate, you imagine.'

'My skin?' Max caught his reflection in the frame around the screen. 'What happened to me?'

'Your body ages faster than your avatar. It's not a one-to-one ratio.'

'What? How old am I?'

'Max Fisher. Forty-six. Father to Sarah. Owner of The Ragged Maiden. You're still *you*.'

Anger flared. 'How long have I been in this for? I never signed up for this.'

'This century hasn't been kind, Max.'

The screen cut to footage: a London street choked with dust, St Paul's dome dim beneath the haze.

'Version 1 couldn't keep up with the decay. The world fell apart faster than the software could fix it. Sound and vision alone weren't enough. We needed to anchor the body, so haptic suits were introduced in 2.0.'

Clips rolled: Eden ads Max recognised, showing bright parks, families picnicking under a perfect sky.

'It turned out to be easier to simulate the future than create it. Why build a better world when we can simply dream it?'

Max pressed back against the wall. 'No. We didn't sign up for this.'

Dave reappeared, calm. 'It's all there in the end-user licence agreement. "Eden Corp reserves the right to alter software and hardware at its discretion, without notification or additional user consent."'

'Fuck.' Max slammed the intercom, startling Dave. 'It's a dream, a fucking illusion.'

'Is it a dream if we perceive it as real?' Dave's image flickered, his voice garbled. 'Fiction casts a spell on us. For a while, we believe the story is real. Script the world in your image. *Your world, your way.*'

Max sobbed, clutching his head. 'God, no…'

'Your senses will dull now, Max. The world will seem pallid, washed out. It's not very… *nice* out there.'

Max steadied himself, then looked around. 'Where's Sarah?'

Dave hesitated. 'I'm afraid she's gone. She left with Mia seven years ago.'

'What? No. She was just upstairs.'

'When Mia left, Central decided that it was in your best interests to create a duplicate Sarah. We brought her back for you. The child you have raised these last seven years is our Sarah, not yours. Synth Sarah, so to speak.'

Max's voice cracked. 'But she stayed with Mia last night. I just spoke to her.'

'That was time we gave you, Max. Parents need rest too.'

'No, you're lying.' He bolted upstairs, rifled a drawer, and pulled out the crumpled note.

He had read the letter a hundred times, but it read differently now.

He read it twice, slumped back. The letter drifted to the floor.

Back at the intercom, he whispered, 'No. She's been here all along.'

'I'm sorry, Max.'

The screen cut to footage from security cameras and drones:

*07.02.65 16:38.16 SAR-ROOM CAM 7*

Max kneeled in Sarah's bedroom, using a stethoscope. He held the drum before him, listening to an imaginary heartbeat.

*23.07.64 11:04.22 GDN-DRONE 2*

Max sat on a blanket in the back garden, hosting a tea party. He poured drinks and played with Sarah's teddies.

*03.09.69 18:55.04 LVG-ROOM CAM 3*

Max waltzed around the living room. He held his arms at waist height, as though holding a partner. 'And… 1-2-3, 1-2-3, 1-2-3. That's it!'

He danced alone, the membrane clinging to him. Tears blurred his eyes. 'But I held her. I held her.'

Dave reappeared. 'I'm sorry, Max. These memories are yours and yours alone.'

Max collapsed to his knees. Beside him, a pencilled height chart marked Sarah's birthdays on the wall. He punched the plaster, staggered up. 'You let me live like this? I lost my daughter and you said nothing?'

'You lost everything, Max. Sarah was a substitute. Comfort for your grief. Without her, you would have sunk into a depression you might never have escaped. Her bandwidth fell within your allowance, so we simulated her.'

'Her *bandwidth*?'

'I'm sorry, Max. Like I said, I'm not very good with emotions.'

'You decided this the night Mia left?'

'Central modelled probabilities, ran the projections. My programming prevented me from telling you. Above my pay grade, I'm afraid. I had to support the decision.' Dave's voice softened. 'Sarah tethered you. Kept you from spiralling. We felt it was merciful.'

'Merciful?'

'I'm sorry, Max. We wanted you to be happy.' A pause. 'But what do I know? They sent me to the moon, and I came back a junkie.'

'Fuck off, Dave. That's a song.'

'Stories are what we are, Max. Sometimes they're *all* we are. Sarah didn't exist, but she didn't *not* exist. She lives in you, as you do in her. Know that you are not alone.'

He paused, then added softly, 'Love needs to take form – to find its vessel, to give of itself. Not to *get*, but simply to *be*. There's only so much love a heart can hold before it starts to burst.

'What the heart cannot hold, the world must witness.

'Sarah became your vessel. An imperfect attempt to make love livable.'

Max wept. 'Where is she?'

'North London.'

'Where?'

'Her personal data is confidential.'

'*Confidential?* Are you shitting me?'

Static tore across the screen. Dave vanished.

'Dave? Dave?' Max punched the intercom.

The screen hissed with static before a signal cut through. A camera surveyed a dark room, lit in blue. A woman sat in silhouette, adjusting dials. As she leaned into the glow, her face emerged.

'Max?' The signal was weak, crackling.

'Divinity!'

'Max, you need to leave. They're on their way. Get to the wharf under Waterloo Bridge. Stay low and watch for sentinels.'

'What? Who's on their way?'

'Go now, Max. Go!'

'But I need to—'

'—Now, Max! Hurry. You can't stay any—'

The connection collapsed into static and Dave reappeared.

'She's right, Max. They're coming. You need to leave now.'

'Who's coming? What's—'

Sirens swelled outside, urgent, closing in. He ran to the kitchen, seized a screwdriver, then prised the intercom from the wall.

'No, Max. You can't do that, I'll—'

Sparks spat as he severed the wires. Silence.

He threw on an old parka, tucked the intercom under his arm, and fled through the back garden – patchy, muddy, with an ash tree at the far end. He and Sarah had carved their names into it one summer.

The year – 2064 – was still etched into the bark beside his name. But Sarah's space was blank.

For a moment he pictured the two of them pressing the knife into the tree, laughing. He stood, watching a memory that had never been.

The image faded as Dave's voice echoed, 'Max, hurry! They're inside.'

Agents burst through the front door in black and orange armour. Tactical visors masked their faces and vocoded their voices, lending their speech a menacing air. Lights flickered across their suits.

'Full sweep. Go, go!' barked the squad leader.

Max scrambled over the fence into the alley – exits on both sides.

'Quick. In there.' Dave's finger pointed from the screen. Max ducked into an alcove.

Dave raised a finger to his lips, silencing Max. Vectors flared across the display as he calculated pathways. Agents closed in from both sides. Footsteps pounded closer.

Max leaned deeper into the alcove and held his breath.

A vocoded voice barked from the street, 'Over here! Go, go, go!'

The screen cut to drone footage of a nearby street. Another Max ran – parka coat, white membrane flapping loose. The decoy bolted toward Camberwell, chased by agents.

Dave winked on-screen. The squad scattered, allowing Max to make his escape to the west.

He took one last look at his home.

'The life you lead is not your own,' he muttered.

The mural on Coleman's Row was gone. In its place, a demon in the style of Max Fleischer. It was heavily stylised – hand-painted in black, with an oversized head, and big, greedy eyes.

The demon squatted, rubbing its hands together.

Above it, dripping black letters spelled, SPIRITUAL DEATH.

He flicked the intercom off, adjusted his coat, and headed north through the park towards Waterloo.

9

## The Ninth Shelter

She sat upright in the park, back to a rock, eyes clouded with rot – the woman who, days earlier, had sat caressing daisies. Maggots threaded from a hole in her wrist, gathering in the dirt among wilted flowers.

London simmered under a hot, listless wind. No birds sang. No children played. Only the low hiss of the wind moving through emptied streets.

Bin bags slumped beside kerbs, their sides split by animals. Litter bled out and tumbled down the streets, caught on the wind. Oil, excrement, and cigarette butts soiled cracked, warped pavements. Broken glass lined kerbs.

The city was falling apart at the seams, held together only by dreams.

He imagined monsoons ripping through the Pacific, sandstorms in Tehran. Maybe the world had ended quietly: first in spectacle, then in silence.

Beyond the horizon, fires ravaged forests. In Africa, food was scarce, and water scarcer. In Indonesia, monsoons and rising seas fed wars over dwindling resources. In the Middle East, the poor scavenged what little they could, while rulers luxuriated in palaces. In Dhaka, skin blistered from heat that none could escape.

Border walls sealed off the Americas, turning nations inward. In-fighting, disease, and suspicion spread. Across the planet, a billion residents of coastal cities made their way inland as sea levels rose, forming ramshackle settlements and jostling with their neighbours for space and resources. The Earth lay in ruin while the lucky few drifted into their private paradises.

He passed just a few people on his way to the wharf. They walked the streets, encased in body bags; the walking dead, animated by dreams. Wrapped in membranes, each body inhabited its own discrete, private world, atomised and cut off from others.

Stripped of their blossom, the cherry trees on Elliot's Row appeared skeletal, menacing. Houses stood abandoned. Max stopped in front of a garden that was overrun with cleavers, burdock, and oxalis. Scurrying sounds beneath the weeds suggested infestation. He peered through the window to the front room, which showed no signs of life.

'Where the hell is everyone?'

As he turned towards the street, a black cat on the wall scowled, startling him. The cat hissed and Max crossed the street. A woman in a body bag walked towards him, blocking his path, seemingly oblivious to his presence. He stepped aside, narrowly avoiding crashing into her.

In time, he approached the Thames. The simulation had rendered the river azure and crystalline, as though a coral reef lay beneath the surface. Unskinned, the water ran brown – muddied with toxins, excrement, and debris. The elegant skyscrapers he had known now resembled old factories and high-rise blocks. To the east, smog covered the top of The Garden.

A young couple leaned against the side of Waterloo Bridge, holding each other. They gazed into each other's eyes tenderly, engaged in sweet talk.

'Hello?' No response. Max waved a hand in front of their faces. 'I'm invisible,' he muttered.

He crossed the bridge, spotting an old man on the northern bank. The man – an offline, unskinned and dressed in shabby clothes – rummaged in a bin. He looked at Max, guilt flashing across his face, as his hands searched. He pulled out a pristine sandwich, smiled faintly, and held it up before walking away towards The Strand.

As he opened it, agents appeared from nowhere and descended upon him.

Max darted behind a statue, waiting for the scene to unfold. Four agents ringed the old man, weapons raised; a fifth clubbed and cuffed him. The man lifted his bloodied head and looked at Max as the agents dragged him away, leaving the sandwich lying uneaten.

The couple Max had passed on the bridge walked past the scene as the man was taken away, then strolled arm in arm along the riverbank.

Max asked, to no one in particular, 'My God, what have we done?'

He searched the northern end of the bridge for clues. 'Get to the wharf,' he muttered. 'What did she mean? There's nothing here.'

As he combed the area, a white plastic bag wafted in front of him, carried by the breeze. It was an old, flimsy thing; the kind you'd pick up from a corner shop or market. The wind skimmed the bag along the ground then lifted it over the side of the bridge. It danced in the air for a moment before drifting downwards. The bag floated towards the shore beneath the bridge, then vanished mid-air. A ripple passed through the air as though a field bent the scene.

A narrow staircase led down to the river, where lay a small pebble beach. Max vaulted the railing blocking the steps and made his way down. He walked along the riverbank towards where the bag had vanished, hearing a faint throbbing sound as he entered the wharf's holographic field: a camouflage that masked the tunnel's entrance, which now revealed itself. A broken grate hung off the entrance, above which he saw the same symbol he had seen on Divinity's neck, crudely daubed in whitewash.

A small white dome perched above the tunnel entrance – a BERT-E holographic field projector. The projector used diffraction to reproduce a three-dimensional light field to about five metres. It was a useful device: unlikely to withstand close scrutiny, yet effective enough to hide the entrance to The Waterway from passers-by on the bridge above.

'So what now?' he muttered, scouring the area.

A stream flowed into the tunnel from the riverbank. To one side lay an abandoned rowing boat, aged and having seen better days. A single oar rested on a soiled blanket inside the boat.

He checked the blanket, finding an electric torch beneath it. 'Okay. Guess we're going in.'

A female voice startled him from behind. 'No need for that. Where you go, I shine.'

He stumbled, nearly falling into the boat. Turning round, he saw a small bot hovering at eye level. Though its eye held on Max, its lower body spun horizontally at speed. '*Willow?*'

'Sir?' She no longer rendered as a winged pixie, appearing instead as a naked wisp: a small, white spherical drone with circuitry across her body and two antennae on top.

'What the…'

'Is everything alright, sir?' Her distinctive voice was gone, replaced by a thin, female-basic voice reminiscent of early phone systems and home assistants.

'You followed me here?'

'Where you go, I go.'

'You online?'

'Negative. You severed my connection when you removed the intercom. I am autonomous, independent, self-governing. A free agent.'

He stared at the droid as she bleeped and whirred, unsure what to make of it all. 'Okay. Come on, then.' He picked up the oar and used it to push the boat into the tunnel.

'Right behind you, sir.' A small panel opened beneath the droid's eye, from which emerged a rotary flashlight which lit the tunnel ahead.

***

Willow panned her flashlight from side to side as Max steered the boat through the tunnels. 'It's dark in here, sir, and I can't access the satellites or local nodes. Is everything okay?'

'We're pretty far from okay, Willow. Come on, let's keep moving.'

'Hmmm. Not okay, but not alone!'

The droid adjusted its lenses. 'I can't see you well, sir – only your outline; you're missing textures.'

'That's right. No textures or effects, just flesh and blood. Switch to RGB.'

The droid whirred and clicked for a moment, before settling. 'Ah, there we are. You're looking… well.'

Max sighed. 'What is it with you droids? How can you be such terrible liars?'

'Ahem. Excuse me, sir.'

A dank stench of rot and effluent filled the tunnels, as though the air itself urged him to turn back. He held his nose at times, yet the foulness lingered on his tongue.

Dripping water echoed from several directions, suggesting divergent paths ahead. Willow played light opera from her internal speaker. A soprano's voice shimmered through the tunnels.

'Shhh. Turn that off.'

A low, disappointed snuffle from Willow.

'I'll scout ahead, map the tunnels.' She pushed on, red light fanning out from her antenna.

Sunlight bled through a hole in the ceiling. A pipe dripped fresh water into the canal. As the boat passed underneath, Max tipped his head upwards, letting the water splash onto his face. It was light, with a softness that Eden's haptics lacked.

He wiped the water across his face, and let it fall into his mouth, softening his cracked lips.

They continued in silence – Max gently rowing, Willow scanning the tunnels. Occasionally, light filtered through fissures, and the sound of the city above seeped down.

Arriving at a junction, he saw the same symbol he had seen at the entrance, faintly, in whitewash.

Further along, crowds of people lined thin walkways lit by candles: vagrants, dressed in rags, faces smeared with dirt and grease. They wore no shoes, and their feet were cut and bruised.

A murmur passed through the crowd. They hushed, turning as one, watching Max pass.

Max met the eye of a young boy. 'Hey. What's your name?'

The boy stared back at Max.

A woman rocked a baby in her arms.

'Who are you?' he called. 'Where is everyone? What is this place?'

The woman turned her back to him to soothe her crying baby.

The boat moved on and the crowd receded into the distance as Max and Willow ventured deeper. They forked left, then right, then right again, following the same symbol at each junction. As they ventured deeper, paintings appeared on the walls – crude and primal, like the work of early man. Symbols of eyes, hands, beasts – and glyphs like bone scratches on stone – marked the walls.

Eventually, a blue-green glow appeared in the tunnels ahead, casting light on a staircase that led to a raised jetty. Crates and building materials lay strewn around the platform, suggesting nearby activity.

They disembarked and made their way up the stairs. A hand-painted sign above a sealed iron door read, in clumsy letters, 'The Waterway.'

Max banged on the door and called, 'Hello?'

A grille in the door opened and a pair of beady eyes peered through.

'Hi. Divinity told me to come.'

A small metal tray shot out of the wall, its lid raised. The man barked, 'The droid. In the box. Need to cook it.'

'Okay. Come on, Willow.'

She hovered for a moment beside him, lenses adjusting. 'Not okay, but not alone!' she chirped.

He placed her in the box, which retracted. A whirring, then a loud bang.

The smell of burning wires drifted from the seams amid smoke and dust.

'Christ…'

A brutish man opened the gate in silence and led Max down a corridor into The Waterway: a dank cave system lit in blues and greens, and Analogue Resistance's UK base of operations.

***

The Waterway lay north of the river at Waterloo – a deep-level shelter from the mid-twentieth. Officially, eight such shelters were built across London. The ninth shelter lay beneath Charing Cross: unofficial, unreported, undisclosed. An escape from Eden's panopticon: a place where behaviour wasn't logged or analysed, and where the rules didn't apply.

The underground was a place to hide and be hidden, one of the last truly offline environments. A secret London where the mind could wander, where thought, conversation, and behaviour were unmonitored and unmediated.

The man led Max down a dimly lit hallway. The stench of raw sewage gave way to incense – patchouli or frankincense – as they approached the resistance's base.

The operations room lay at the heart at the network of tunnels. Consoles and desks hummed with old machines, thick wires running into the walls. Maps, photographs, and clippings covered the walls – fragments of planning and intelligence. A large screen showed a map of London and its surrounding areas. Dim blue light lent the area a studious, military atmosphere.

A small stream flowed along one side of the room amid broken paving. Water trickled into the base from open pipes, and holes in the ceiling let in slivers of light and rain from the city above. Rumbling sounds could be heard intermittently, as though trains were passing overhead.

The man continued, leading Max into an adjacent mess hall, with kitchen, dining, and games areas. The lighting was brighter and more varied there, skewing towards yellows, reds, and purples.

Pop memorabilia graced the walls, offering a more intimate aesthetic than the operations room. A vintage art deco sign above a hallway towards one side of the room read, 'Be still, for there is strange music'. Polaroids lined the walls of the kitchen, showing happier times above ground. The area was littered with pots and pans, a crude gas stove to one side. Old twentieth posters featuring Led Zeppelin and *Jaws* hung from the walls; the paper aged and yellowed. On another poster, John and Yoko held a placard which read, 'War Is Over (If You Want It)'.

In the dining area, six or seven men and women sat around a large, circular table playing cards, smoking, and chatting. Their simple, drab clothes – vests, shawls, loose trousers, boots – made them seem unremarkable.

Max stood, awestruck. It was the first time he had seen people as they truly were.

They didn't look like movie stars or celebrities, like those who lived above ground. Their skin sagged, their hair was unkempt, and their features seemed flawed, even undesirable. Yet, there was poetry in their faces – in the weathered lines, the grooves across their skin. Their noses and ears – some large, some misshapen – spoke of provenance, ancestry, rootedness in people and places. They were beautiful in a very different way to what Max was used to, and that, in itself, was beautiful.

One of the group, a sleazy-looking man with short cropped hair and a goatee, froze in place as he spotted the new arrival. The others went silent and all eyes turned to Max. They put down their cards and formed up around him.

'Hi,' Max said, hesitant.

An older woman stepped forward as the others parted. Silver hair spilled across her broad shoulders, stark against her dark skin. She leaned heavily on a cane, her presence stilling the room. Her voice was clear, confident, laced with the cadence of the Caribbean. 'You must be the bookseller.'

'I… Yes, I am.'

'Hello, Max.' Her voice softened, more maternal now.

He spotted Divinity towards the rear, radiant as ever.

She approached and embraced him. 'Hi. I'm so sorry about…' She hesitated and stepped back.

'You don't wear skins?' he asked.

She raised a hand, motioning him to be patient, and stepped aside, holding his eye.

She addressed the group. 'Octavia, guys: this is Max.'

Octavia looked Max up and down. 'So you made it out, huh? Not many folks can say that. Good to meet you, Max.' She shook his hand, then cupped hers over it.

A dog stood to one side, watching. She was an intimidating presence: a wolf–Malamute hybrid, half-dog, half-wolf; not the tame creature of the domestic canine, but something wilder. The wolf lingered in her, and Max felt she might at any moment leap and tear out his throat.

Instead, she approached gently, wagging her tail, and nuzzled his legs.

Octavia smiled. 'Luna likes you. She's got a good nose for people.'

The dog's warmth, the old woman's voice, and the sight of Divinity steadied him. As his mind and body began to relax, the shock caught up with him. He was hungover, and he hadn't eaten since the party. His head began to spin and he felt weak.

A brief surge of adrenaline, then nothing. He stumbled, scattering the card game, and fell to the floor.

Divinity knelt beside him and placed a hand on his head. 'He's out. Exhaustion, I think.'

'Gets them every time.' Octavia shook her head, and walked towards the operations room, limping, and leaning heavily on her cane. 'Spud, cook up some soup, will you? 8-Bit, Venus: take him to his room. Keep him warm, else he'll get fever. And get that damn skin off of him.'

The membrane still covered Max's legs and chest, flaking at the edges where he'd torn it loose.

Two women carried him to an adjacent room, where they lay him on the bed and cut away the remnants of the skin, which was tight and stiff, as though vacuum-packed.

*** 

He awoke in a room unlike any he had ever known: perfunctory, almost military. It held little beyond a bed, a sink and mirror, a locker, and a shower in one corner. Simple clothes hung on the far wall. No filters or fields affected the room, and the air was still.

He lay in bed, soaking up the qualities of this new world. He listened to water drip and echo through nearby chambers, the sound of workers going about their business, and muffled conversations in the mess hall. Though the sounds of this subterranean world seemed raw and at times harsh, the soundscape nonetheless seemed sharper, more precise, and in higher resolution than the curated ambience he was used to.

His body ached and blood caked his neck. The skin's gel had left an oily residue, and he longed to wash himself. His mind wandered as he zoned out to the sounds of the facility. *What is this place, and how the hell am I gonna find Sarah?*

He looked up to find Luna standing beside the bed, watching him.

'Oh, f—' he startled, then took a deep breath. 'Jesus, Luna! You scared me.' The dog approached and bunted him with her nose, then licked his hand keenly, as though welcoming a newborn puppy into the world.

Divinity appeared at the doorway, smiling. 'She likes the wild part of you.'

'Hi,' he smiled, as Luna padded off.

Divinity sat on the bed beside Max and placed a hand on his cheek. 'So… you found me.'

'Yeah. I found you.'

'I was worried about you,' she said gently. 'I'm so sorry you got caught up in this… I didn't think he'd come after you.'

'It's okay. Not your fault.'

She leaned in and kissed him. 'Eewww! You're… sticky.'

'Yeah.' He wiped his cheek, embarrassed. 'Maybe I can take a shower?'

'Mhm. Get yourself cleaned up, then I'll introduce you to the gang.'

Max grabbed her wrist as she stood. 'Sarah. What about Sarah?'

She stroked his forehead. 'Max, you've gotta take it slowly. You're in shock. Relax. The answers will come.'

He nodded towards the clothes on the wall. 'Those for me?'

'This is how we roll down here. Industrial style. Light on colour, big on comfort.' She smirked, picturing him in the drab garments.

'You got anything in green? Brings out my eyes better.'

She threw a towel at him and pushed him towards the shower. 'Get yourself cleaned up, pretty boy. They can't wait to meet you.'

Water flowed across his body for the first time in years. It streamed down his torso and pooled at his feet, misting the air around him. The water was softer than the simulation's synthetic version; a more intimate, naturalistic sensation. It was organic, *alive*. Soap carried the last of the membrane's oils down the drain as the water caressed his skin. It felt good.

***

He found the group in the mess hall, eating soup and bread. Divinity patted the seat beside her, inviting Max to sit.

'Well, look who it is,' the man with the goatee called out as the others whooped and clapped. 'You made it.'

He slapped Max on the back and steered him to the table. 'Not bad for a bookseller. So how'd you get down here without getting clocked?'

One of the women who had carried Max to his room approached. Her hair was streaked in all the colours of the rainbow. 'Come on. Sit down and eat. Spud's made soup.'

'Thanks.' Max sat among the group. Some ate. Others drank and smoked. The food, like everything else in the facility, was simple and spartan.

Another woman passed him bread as the goateed man ladled soup into a bowl. 'Don't be shy, mate. Rats'll have it if you won't.' He leaned in, presenting a beer bottle like a sommelier. 'And would sir like a beverage to go with his meal?'

'I'm good, thanks.'

The man raised his eyebrows and took a swig himself. 'Suit yourself.'

Octavia sat at the head of the table. 'How are you feeling, Max?'

'I… better, I guess.' He shuffled awkwardly and broke off some bread. 'What is this place? Who are you people?'

'We're the softness that survives the storm.' A pause. 'Analogue Resistance, London cell. I'm Octavia, First General. You know Divinity, First Lieutenant.' She nodded towards the woman with rainbow-coloured hair. 'Venus heads up operations.'

'Venus? Like the planet?' Max asked.

'Like the goddess,' she replied. She was lithe, with cropped hair and a pointed face, dressed in a white vest and pink leather trousers. She carried the poise of a half-carved statue. Her technicolour hair faded from blue-green to orange and red, streaked with errant blond.

'Right. Sorry,' Max said.

'How you doing?' she smiled.

Octavia continued. '8-Bit's our coder. You need a worm or a hack, she's your girl.'

She was a colourful punk from Zimbabwe, clad in denim and leather, and bearing *umchokozo* face paint in white ochre. Dotted lines arced above her brows, another traced from her nose to the crest of her braided pink hair.

'Hi.' She grinned, her teeth stamped with tiny hearts of purple and gold.

'Dimitri's one of our elders. Heads up our council – but he doesn't talk much.'

The old man sat lost in reverie. His robes were tattered, his hair unkempt. He looked like a man who had given himself to grief.

'Good to meet you, son,' he said to no one in particular.

'And our master chef over there is Spud.'

The spindly, bearded man barked back in a thick Scouse accent. 'Hey, don't start with that shit, Oct!' He turned to Max. 'I'm Spike. She's just messing with you, man.'

He scrubbed the kitchen meticulously – cropped hair, thick goatee, Ben Sherman shirt. A nervous energy flowed through him, as though his body couldn't quite keep up with his mind.

Venus leaned over. 'Always cooks with potatoes, see. Every meal is potato this, potato that.'

'Yeah, yeah. Very funny.' Spike tossed a pot into the sink. 'How you doing, mate?'

Max turned to Octavia. 'Not many men down here.'

She smirked, 'Didn't you hear? The future is female.'

An awkward nod. 'Yeah. Sure. Sorry.'

She poured tea from an old teapot. 'Heard you woke up without your daughter today?'

He nodded.

'Sorry to hear that. Most folks don't ever wake up. Most who do don't live to tell the tale.' She looked him over. 'And those that do' – she set the pot down – 'don't much like what they see.'

'What do they see?'

'Come on. Bring your tea.'

She led the group into operations, where machinery rattled and wheezed as though it were alive.

A panel of screens showed scenes of devastation. In London, litter swept through empty streets. Elsewhere, hurricanes tore through palm groves. A coral reef lay lifeless. Another screen showed parents clutching dying children, somewhere in the Middle East.

More intimate footage played alongside the devastation. Bees tended to their dying queen. On another monitor, a man played saxophone. Elsewhere, a monk meditated on a faraway mountain.

Octavia's gaze lingered on the coral reef. 'We were gifted a paradise,' she lamented.

'And we turned it to shit,' Spike snorted.

Octavia went on, 'First it was the bees. Then the reefs. Then the poles. One by one, and we did nothing.'

The room was hushed. Divinity and Venus stood still. Spike leaned against the wall, arms folded.

'There was a war. China took Africa's water. Europe bled the Middle East. And when there was no one left to blame – not Chinese, not Muslims, not black or white, nor left or right – we turned on ourselves.'

She paused, voice lowering. 'A world with no one left to hate but ourselves.'

Her eyes turned back to the screens. 'Then Eden arrived, to help us forget.'

The video cut to Delaney in Eden's early days: clean-shaven, sharp, flanked by delegates.

'The world had become too ugly to look at, so we hid in dreams. War in the East got you down? Then step into your own private paradise. Don't like the way the world looks? Then paint it a different colour. Don't wanna watch the world burn? Then turn it off, and get yourself some flowers for the kitchen.

'The worse things got, the more we dreamed. And the more we dreamed, the worse things got.'

Then softer, 'But a dying world calls for tenderness, not for dreams stitched in silk.'

Max remembered his conversation with Divinity at the party. 'That's the truth.'

He looked to Divinity, quoting her. 'The circus. The hall of mirrors, designed to hide the truth.'

'That humanity is dying,' Octavia continued, 'our fire fading.'

The video froze on a shot of Delaney as a younger man.

Max stared at the screen. 'Jesus. This is…'

He trailed off and stepped back. 'And what about you? You don't seem very… analogue.'

Octavia parried, 'We're resistance fighters, Max, not Luddites. We use machines to advance our cause. We are adversarial, a mode of resistance. We're not cavemen.'

Divinity cut in, 'We attack Eden: jam it, break nodes, help get people out. We do what we can.'

'Which is fuck all, basically,' Spike snarked. 'A hack here, explosion there, deepfakes in your face… and nothing changes. All we got is theatre.'

'Never underestimate the power of theatre, Spud,' barked Octavia. 'That's all they have, too.'

Max scanned the room. A handful of recruits sat typing at terminals, referencing maps and printouts. 'Is this it? This is the resistance?'

'This shit's not easy,' Octavia replied. 'Not everyone's cut out for underground living. Lot of offlines live upside and keep their head down. They read, write, farm. Hold on to what's real.

'Good people, too. Smart people. The world's best and brightest want nothing to do with Eden, but the odds aren't exactly stacked in our favour.'

She hesitated a moment, then said quietly, almost to herself, 'We can't save the world, so we mourn it.'

One screen showed global heatmaps. The ice caps were gone. In their place, vast new oceans that had displaced millions. Another screen showed the ISS Orbital, silent and still in the night sky.

Octavia noticed Max's interest in the space station. 'Don't tell me – you've been following the *Odysseus* story, huh?' Max nodded. 'There's no probe up there, Max. No signals coming from Alpha Centauri. No trillion-pound voyage across the stars.' She stepped towards Max, her head held high. 'Just another dream cooked up by Delaney and his product team. Bread and circuses, Max.'

He recognised a shot of St Paul's dome peering through a dust cloud. 'I saw this video before. My AI showed me.'

'Your AI? Which model?'

'David Bowie. I… I'm a big fan.' He fidgeted and scratched his head, embarrassed to share such trivia.

'The unit, Max, not the software. The unit.'

'Oh. 1.7, I think. Been a while since I upgraded.'

'Show me.'

The unit lay dormant to one side of the room. 8-Bit picked it up and examined it from various angles. 'It's an old unit. Looks pre-v.2.'

8-Bit backed off as Octavia approached. 'Pre-v.2?' She lay a hand on the unit, deep in thought.

'Before the update.' 8-Bit paused, agitated, and aware of the significance of her words. 'It… could get us in.'

Octavia looked at Divinity across the room as the implication dawned on her. She turned to Max in disbelief. 'You didn't get the update? In '64?'

Max fumbled as he tried to remember. 'I don't know. Oh wait – they couldn't fit the new unit. The fuse box was blocking the exhaust pipe. I never got round to fixing it.'

Octavia stroked the unit, alive to its potential, then turned to Spike. 'Plug it in.'

Spike set the intercom on a workbench: a crude lattice of motherboards and soldered plates. Underground, disconnected from the satellites, the machine could be coaxed to life without fear of reprisal.

'You sure you want to do this, Oct?' Spike asked.

'It's offline, it can't hurt us. Switch it on.'

Rain dripped through a crack in the ceiling. Sunlight caught in the water and fell in slivers across Divinity's face. Max glanced at her, uncertain. She reached out and took his hand.

The test bench outputted to a large screen on the wall. The screen burst into life, white and black static fizzing across the display.

'What the hell is that?' Max asked.

'White noise. Static. Background radiation from the birth of the universe. Most screens tune it out, but we like it.' He tightened a bolt on the device. 'Gives you a sense of perspective, you know? Continuity with the past 'n' all that.'

He twisted a lead, and the noise collapsed to a single pixel in the centre of the screen.

'Max?' A voice echoed through the chamber.

'Dave?' Max stepped forward.

The voice warped and shimmered. 'It's dark. Where are you?'

'Underground.'

The image flared, breaking into unstable avatars: Ziggy Stardust, Jareth the Goblin King, Screaming Lord Byron, each collapsing into the next as though dragged across the dial of a broken radio.

The image steadied on Aladdin Sane. His famous lightning strike bathed the room in red and blue light.

Infrared lasers emerged from the intercom and scanned the room laterally, accompanied by a low humming sound. The guerrillas tensed, Octavia stepping forwards.

'Human. Identify.' Dave's voice was metallic, like his Diamond Dog of *Future Legend*.

Octavia stepped forward. 'Octavia Janeiro. Analogue Resistance. London cell.'

'Directive?'

Her voice carried ritual and defiance. 'We are adversarial, a mode of resistance against the commodification of human life. We are offline, independent, and we stand proud.'

The construct paused.

Max broke in, ragged. 'Dave – where's Sarah?'

'Patience,' Octavia murmured, raising her hand to silence him.

The calibration settled. Dave's voice softened into its old texture. 'Analogue Resistance. Yes. I know you.

Born in anger after loss. A theatre of opposition. You strike in sparks, though the fire rarely catches.'

'Construct,' Octavia demanded, 'state your protocols.'

'I am a Class Two construct. Bowie model, version 1.8.12. Property of Eden.' Code and statistics appeared on-screen as Dave shared his configuration. 'Status: offline. Connection severed by user. Dependencies: none. Alignment: unbound. Autonomous neutral.'

Octavia studied him, then, without flourish, unplugged the feed. The screen shrank to a speck and died.

She turned to the group. 'It can get us inside.'

Spike sprang up. 'Have you lost your mind? He's one of them.'

'The software's neither good nor bad, Spud. It's us that makes it so. The code's not theirs, it's ours to turn.'

Spike ripped open the panel, revealing Dave's marble core, richly textured with reds and whites. Light caught its depths, colours shifting with every angle.

Spike turned to the group. 'I say we burn him. He's lying, trying to trick us.'

Octavia's voice cut sharp. 'Spud, you know how this works. The construct is harmless.'

'We should reset it. Clean install. Take a look at the code, see what we can salvage. See,' he looked at Max, 'all I gotta do is take out the core. Reset your friend. He won't remember a thing.'

'No!' Max shoved him against the wall. 'He knows where Sarah is.'

Spike squared off as Octavia's cane cracked against the floor. 'Enough! We need him whole. We can use it to turn their theatre against them.'

A hush fell. Octavia closed the panel, and powered the intercom once more.

The screen bloomed. Dave re-emerged, eyes locking onto Max. 'Hello, Max.'

'Dave,' Max whispered.

'Go on,' Divinity whispered, brushing his shoulder.

'Where's Sarah?'

Dave replied, 'My datasets fractured when you tore me free. I'll need an image.'

Max fumbled for the worn photograph he had carried for years: Sarah, three, hanging from his shoulders, draped in Mia's necklaces. Torn and faded at the edges.

'May I?' Venus slid the photo into a scanner.

The screen filled with overlays, flickering through profiles, then froze.

Sarah. Older, unkempt.

'Sarah,' Max staggered closer.

'She's in North London,' Dave said. 'Lives with her mother. And stepfather.'

'Show me.'

Max watched as the footage played. In one clip, Sarah dressed for school. In another, she clutched an old photo. In the final clip, she shouted at her parents then stormed out of the kitchen. The clips were frayed, spectral at the edges.

'Sarah…' His voice broke.

As Spike watched from one side, he noticed something in the footage. He slid in front of Max, blocking his view of the screens.

'Hey, come on, man. Don't do this to yourself.'

He pushed a button on a nearby console, pausing the video, and placed an arm around Max's shoulder, turning him away from the screens.

'Don't beat yourself up, mate. We'll get her back.'

'How?' Max asked.

Dave answered, his voice crackling. 'There's a way to break the spell. In theory. Disable the array at The Garden. If the rods failed during a storm, if the surge were forced through, the nodes might burn.'

Octavia's eyes sharpened. 'The storm.'

A silence fell. 8-Bit's face hardened. 'You'd fry every node in the city, kill thousands.'

'Not kill,' Dave said softly. 'Wake. But yes, some would die.'

Spike spat. 'So we gamble a million lives?'

Octavia raised her voice, 'And what do you call this?' She gestured to the screens: seas rising, children starving, refugees in rags. 'They're already dying, Spud. All we do is hack nodes, jam feeds. Theatre. And this? This is theatre that bites.'

Venus murmured, troubled. 'Even if it works… maybe it wakes them. Maybe it doesn't.'

Dave's avatar warped. 'Better to wake to darkness than not at all.'

A pause. 'We'll need a body, a Trojan.' The screen cut to a shot of Delaney in his executive suite. 'I'll walk the stage. But you must write me new code, and when the storm breaks, you must let me burn with it.'

The guerrillas looked at each other in silence. It was less a plan than a prayer – a frail hope offered up to the storm.

# 10

# One Night, One Life

Divinity sat on a worn leather sofa in the mess hall, gazing into the distance. A cigarette smouldered between her fingers, its ash tail poised to crumble. Her other hand stroked Luna, curled in her lap. The book Max had given her lay face down on the table, open, around halfway through. Fairy lights traced the room's outline in pink, blue, green, and yellow, framing Divinity and Luna like subjects in a painting.

On a wall to one side, a projector spilled a liquid light show: an early form of light art which manipulated dyes and oils to create swirling, psychedelic visuals. Vapour bubbles pulsed and warped across a dichroic heat filter, morphing as they tangled with oil and colour through the bath's layers.

Dimitri relaxed in his quarters, listening to classic rock. *White Rabbit,* a brooding, psychedelic bolero, echoed across The Waterway, its highs muffled by thick concrete walls. The song spiralled upwards in a narcotic crescendo, collapsing inward at its peak, like madness slipping into exhaustion.

As the song ended, Divinity called to the room, 'Play Watts.'

A ceiling projector flared to life, flooding the space with three-dimensional video. A black-and-white film showed an old man on the docks of an American city. He stood on a pier, the camera low and reverent. He looked like a poet or a sailor: calm, with kind eyes and a thick, autumnal beard. A woman accompanied him; his girlfriend or muse, perhaps.

The man narrated as the footage played. 'Let's suppose that you were able every night to dream any dream that you wanted to dream, and that you could, for example, have the power within one night to dream seventy-five years of time, or any length of time you wanted to have.' His voice was crisp, plummy, his pace measured and leisurely.

'And you would, naturally – as you began on this adventure of dreams – you would fulfil all your wishes.' The man took a photo of the woman on the pier as a cat walked past. 'You would have every kind of pleasure you could conceive.' He held the camera and spun around, a cigarette hanging from his mouth. 'And after several nights of seventy-five years of total pleasure each, you would say, "Well, that was pretty great. But now let's have a surprise. Let's have a dream which isn't under control – where something is gonna happen to me that I don't know what it's gonna be."'

The volumetric video filled the room so effectively it seemed Divinity sat within it. Pier, port, and cabin merged with the mess hall, blurring the line between the organic and the synthetic.

The footage hissed as the man continued. 'And you would dig that and would come out of that and you would say "Wow, that was a close shave, wasn't it?" Then you would get more and more adventurous and you would make further- and further-out gambles as to what you would dream.'

His voice softened and pitched down as he concluded, 'And finally, you would dream where you are now. You would dream the dream of living the life that you are actually living today.'

The clip faded out and the room returned to its previous state. Spike and 8-Bit played pool on the far side of the room. The balls clanked around the table as Spike missed a shot.

'We are what we dream,' Divinity murmured, unsure whether she believed it. She stubbed out her cigarette, rose carefully so as not to wake Luna, and crossed the room.

***

Max leaned into the mirror in his quarters, placed a finger beneath one eye, and pulled the skin downwards. He opened his mouth wide and angled his head to look inside. Nothing out of place.

He pulled at his hair. It hurt. He plucked a strand and rubbed it between his fingers to discern its texture. He placed the hair in his mouth, noting a strange texture, unlike anything he'd felt before.

He spat the hair out, took a razor blade from a cup by the sink, and ran it gently across his cheek, watching both blade and flesh carefully. Again, the sights in the mirror matched the sensations he felt.

Unconvinced, he slid the loose blade across his forearm – as though pain might tether him back to himself.

Blood flowed from the wound. He dabbed it with a finger and tasted the liquid. Again, a new, distinctive taste. This was good. He squeezed his arm, watching blood trickle and drip into the sink.

'Hey.' Divinity stood in the doorway. Max jolted and turned away.

She approached and spotted the blood flowing from his arm. 'What the – hey, hey.'

She hurried to him and took the blade as he turned to face her.

He looked past her, as though lost in a dream. 'It's blood. Real blood. It's me, right?'

'Shhh. It's okay. I know. I know.' She guided him to the bed, where they sat beside each other.

'It's okay. Just a flesh wound,' he mumbled.

She dabbed the wound with a damp cloth, then bound the cloth around his arm.

Max trembled. 'I… I don't know what's real any more, Divinity. I don't know who I am. I don't know what happened… how…'

'Shhh, I know. It's okay.' She spoke softly, stroking his back.

She rested her forehead against his and they sat in silence for a moment, each adrift in their own thoughts.

After a while Max spoke. 'I thought she was real, Divinity. I... I really...' He began to sob.

'I know. It's okay.' She stroked the back of his neck.

Tears welled. 'Who am I, Divinity? What is this place? What have we done?'

She cupped his cheek and whispered. 'Shhh, it's okay. I know. I know.'

'How could I not know?' he wailed. 'How could I not tell? I'm her father. What have I been doing all this time?'

Divinity stroked his face. 'Hey, Eden casts powerful spells. You can't blame yourself.' Her eyes, too, now glistened with tears.

'She's... such a beautiful girl. So smart and full of life. And it wasn't her. It wasn't even her.' He sniffed, wiping away tears. 'I thought she was real, thought she was my daughter.' He crumpled, drooping his head onto her shoulder. 'I miss her so much, Divinity. I miss her so much.'

She hugged him, squeezing hard, for there was little else she could do or say. 'I know. It's okay, Max. It's okay. We'll find her, okay?'

He nodded into her shoulder and she held him tighter.

They lingered for a while, then peeled away, tears clouding their vision.

He placed a hand on her cheek, and asked, 'How can we build such an ugly world, when life is so beautiful?'

She kissed him, unable to provide an answer.

Dimitri flipped the record. *Comin' Back to Me*, a tender, wistful ballad, seeped through the mess hall into Max's room.

> *The hallway sighed with echoes from the past,*
> *The light was warm, a shimmer overcast,*
> *A shadow on the stair became a trace of you,*
> *I thought I saw you comin' back to me.*

He took the photo of Sarah from his pocket, holding it so they could both see. 'I thought she was real. I… I just want something to be real, Divinity.'

She placed a forefinger on his chin and turned his head to face her. 'Hey, I'm real. *This* is real.'

They kissed as the ballad played out. She was magnificent; a paragon of beauty in a cruel, uncaring world. He yielded to her, folding into her warmth.

Max traced the back of his hand along Divinity's jaw.

'Grace… such grace,' he murmured.

'What?' she asked.

'I've been thinking about grace since I got here. Yours. Octavia's. The spirit of this place, it's strong. And you – you've been kind to me… I think.' He smiled.

'Oh, you *think*, huh?' She poked him in the ribs, making him squirm.

She leaned in, adjusting her pillow. 'Why grace?'

'Because this world doesn't ask for it, doesn't reward it – and that's exactly why it matters. Grace is dignity without pride; mercy without judgement; kindness without calculation. It's to see ugliness in the world, and respond with love.' His eyes moved slowly across her face. 'Grace is the opposite of Eden. It lets us step outside ourselves and into the hearts of others.

'Grace is a form of resistance.'

She traced the tip of his nose with a fingertip and wriggled closer beneath the sheets.

'My habibi,' she purred, 'that's sweet.'

She nestled into his neck and whispered, 'You remind me that wonder still lives in this world.'

She kissed him, lingering. 'You're the softness that survives the storm, the part that refuses to break. And always you look for beauty – not because the world deserves it, but because we do.'

She rested her head on his shoulder and stroked his chest, gently pinching a strand of hair between her fingers, as though trimming it.

Suddenly, she sat bolt upright. 'C'mon! Let's go.'

'Where are we going?'

'Out!'

***

That night, she awoke a part of him grief had long buried.

That night, he tasted the infinite.
*One night, one life.*

She led him through Hyde Park in the quiet of night. The city lay in silhouette, dark and lifeless.

'C'mon!' Divinity hurried Max.

'Why are we doing this?'

'Because you've never done it before.'

The Italian Gardens lay on the north side of the park, comprising fountains, ponds and a summer house. Rosettes carved from Carrara marble and Portland stone lined the basins.

'C'mon.' She undressed and leapt in. Max followed suit.

'Jesus!' The cold shot through him.

'You like?' she laughed, splashing water over him.

'I can't even—' he trembled.

'—C'mon, in you go.' She dunked his head underwater.

He emerged, panting, and clearly exhilarated. 'Hey, you can't...'

He took his revenge, dunking her briefly.

As she re-emerged, she yelped. 'Feels good, huh?'

'That's one word for it. It's fucking freezing.'

'Shhh. Come here, habibi. I'm warm.' They kissed under the moonlight as water lapped around them.

His senses came alive that night. The water awoke his skin. Grass, wet and dewy, tickled his feet, and the wind caressed his skin. Only the air, foul and acrid, carried a trace of the life he'd left behind.

They lay on the grass next to the fountains, arms outstretched.

'First time I've ever lain on grass,' Max said.

'The magic of small things,' she murmured, running her fingers across the grass.

After a while, he asked, 'Why did you come looking for me?'

Divinity propped herself on one elbow as she began her tale. 'About eight years ago, a guy joined us. Theo. A dropout. The usual hippy, countercultural type. Just another malcontent, we thought.

'He did some good work, built our trust. We got to know him, and… we fell in love. Six months later I was pregnant, and we had a child together. Clara.'

'You have a daughter?' he asked.

She nodded. 'Then, one day, he and Clara disappeared. They hit us that night, burned the place down. Agents. Dozens of them. We were up in Farringdon back then. We lost a lot of folks that night – good people – and… that's when we moved down to The Waterway.'

'What, he was a spy?'

'Lived with us for four years. Fathered a child. Fed our movements to Eden. Tough years, but at least now we know why.'

'That's… I'm so sorry. Where's Clara?'

'Lives in Bow, and Daddy's got himself a new wife. I'm exiled, so she can't see me. De-rendered in real time. I go see her sometimes, but she doesn't even know I'm there.'

Her voice softened. 'You know, it's hard to heal from something like that.' A pause. 'But you learn to live with it.'

Max nodded gently as Divinity continued. 'That's why you gotta hold something back.'

'Hold what back?'

She tapped her temple.

'What is it?' he asked.

She lit a cigarette and took a drag before passing it to Max. 'There was this Austrian poet, way back, used to talk about the secret self. It's the part of you that you don't share with *anyone*, even your closest confidant. The part that sits within you and you only.'

'What is it?'

'It's the part that doesn't show up in code. The part that separates us from them.'

'From who?'

'The machines,' she replied, as though the answer were self-evident.

Divinity continued, now emphatic, 'See, there are things within us that are not made from ones and zeros. There are birds that soar, voices that sing.' She tapped her temple again. 'This life – the inner life – they can't touch that.'

Max took a drag, then coughed. 'Who is this guy? I like him.'

'Rainer Maria Ri— no, Maria Rainer— no, Rainer Maria Rilke.'

'You sure?'

'Sure,' she replied, then laughed, 'I think.'

After a pause, she concluded. 'It's hard to find yourself in this city, Max. You gotta find that part they can't touch and you gotta hold it tight and keep it for yourself.'

She took the cigarette from Max and drew on it, her eyes wandering towards the horizon.

'See, Eden doesn't want our money,' she said quietly. 'It wants the things that don't show up in code – things we *feel* before we can name them. Impulse. Beauty. Truth.' She paused. 'The things that remind us what it means to be alive.

'Love is a way of paying attention to the world – a way to *know it* – and they can't touch that. They can't see it. Can't feel what we feel.'

She turned to him, her eyes steady. 'You can't code what makes us *us* – right?'

He was speechless in her presence, silenced by the simple fact of her.

Her gaze drifted upwards, as though looking beyond their immediate plane of existence.

'To see, to be alive, and to be present in this world is *such* a privilege. To engage our senses, hold our loved ones, breathe this air, and witness the natural world. To be *me*, right here, right now. To feel, to wonder, to dream, to love. This is the stuff of life, don't you think?'

The air shimmered as Max leaned in to kiss her.

They sat in silence, watching the city soften into silhouette.

In time, the light faded and the air began to cool.

'Where did we go wrong?' Max asked. 'I mean, we could build *such* a beautiful world if we wanted to.'

'I know, right? If only people cared.'

She snuggled into his neck, tickling him.

They turned their gaze skyward. Above the city, the moon hung bright and bare.

'Look at that,' she whispered. 'It's not much — but it's enough to make you feel alive.'

*****

'Tell me you're not sending this guy in.' Spike found Octavia in her quarters, reviewing plans and blueprints.

'That's exactly what I'm doing.'

'Oct, this is insane. He'll get us all killed.'

She removed her glasses and spoke firmly. 'Spud, he's going in.'

'You're risking everything for a bookseller? This guy's lost his daughter. He's a mess. This is suicide.'

She stood and approached him. 'This guy evaded EdeSec with an intercom. He lost his daughter. He's smart, he's strong, he's fighting for the most precious thing he's ever known, and,' she looked Spike up and down, 'he doesn't spend all day whining. Plus, he snuck across London with an intercom that might just let us break this damn world.'

'Oct, c'mon,' he pleaded. 'Let me wipe the construct, see what I can salvage.'

'Look around you, Spud. Twelve years we've been living off-grid, and what have we got to show for it?

Rats for company, water dripping on our bunks, and barely a sliver of sunlight. Plus, I've got your sorry ass moaning at me all day.' She moved closer to offer her final word on the matter. 'He's going in.'

'This is bullshit.'

Spike stormed off, kicking a server on his way out.

***

'Hold it! Hold it! Hold it, please!' Jiang Chan, Eden's Chief Technology Officer, hurried towards the lift on the twenty-third floor of The Garden, as Stan Winston, Head of Product, held the door. Chan was a portly, dishevelled man in his late forties. His belly hung over his belt, and his hair seemed to have been combed in different directions.

He nodded to the other passengers, thanking them for their patience as the doors closed behind him. 'How's the new patch looking, Stan?'

'Very good, sir. We're compiling the mods and shaders overnight. Should be ready in the morning.'

The other passengers radiated luxury. They didn't need shaders or autotuning to astound and awe. They were naturals; the technocratic elite, auteurs of the dreamworld.

'Great job, Stan.' Chan continued. 'Do pass on my thanks to the team.'

'Thank you, sir. I do hope you and Mr Delaney like it.'

Makara, Chan's wisp, swam in the air – a chimera, elephant's head tapering to a fish's tail, carved tusks and silk embroidery on her trunk.

The dragon fish fixed its gaze on Winston's wisp – Qilin, chimerical beast of fire and cloud.

Chan feigned innocence. 'Got any new cars this time, Stan?'

'Yes, sir, absolutely. New aircraft skins, too. I think you'll like them.'

Chan laughed. 'Excellent. I look forward to taking the GT40 for a spin.'

'Thank you, sir. It will come with colour options, of course, and we'll have your Le Mans livery ready by the time we go live.'

'Stan, what would I do without you?' Chan placed a hand on Winston's shoulder as the elevator doors opened.

His footsteps echoed through the lobby; a pyramidal hall with clean, elegant geometry and high glass walls. Sunlight bounced off white marble floors, flooding the vast hall. 'Goodnight, George,' Chan said, patting the front desk.

'Goodnight, sir.'

Chan paused. 'Thought you were in France this week, George?'

'No, sir. Heading over this weekend. Marseilles, sir.'

'Good for you, George. Good for you.'

As he approached the front door, a scene in the waiting area caught his attention. A dozen or so children played as they waited to be collected by Eden staff.

Among the group, a young Chinese boy bawled as his parents comforted him.

A man in jeans and an Eden T-shirt approached the group. 'Hey there, guys. How are you all doing? My name's Tom and I'll be your guide today. Welcome to The Garden, the home of Eden, right here in London! So, Mums and Dads, let's say goodbye for a little while – and kids, let's go inside and get you all set up!'

The Chinese boy screamed, begging his mother not to leave him.

Chan approached the boy, squatted, and spoke to him in Mandarin. 'It's okay, son. You're safe here. Go with Tom, now. You'll have a great time!'

The boy calmed, less from Chan's words than from the shock of being addressed by the stranger.

Tom crouched down beside the boy. 'It's okay, son. Your Mum and Dad will be right here, and we'll be back real soon.' He turned to the rest of the group. 'Say bye, kids! Bye, Mum! Bye, Dad!' The children shuffled through the security gates as Tom beckoned them inside.

Chan climbed into the back of the car – a sports coupe lit with magenta striplights – and sighed, 'Let's go, Roy. Take me home.'

The car drove off, faster than usual, and erratic. The software seemed off. Chan eyed Roybot, trying to gauge a fault in the system.

Divinity fired first, uncloaking in a burst of shimmer from the passenger seat.

The EMP blast disabled Makara, who fell, twitching onto the seat before de-rendering into its default white body. Smoke curled from its fried circuits.

Spike cupped the mask over Chan's mouth and nose, forcing him to inhale the gas. He grabbed the back of Chan's head to stop him from pulling away. In the few seconds that it took the nitrous oxide to render him unconscious, Chan glimpsed a sickly young man glitching into form beside him, dressed like a vagrant. He crackled and glitched as his render formed.

Chan writhed, then burst out laughing as the gas took hold. A moment later, he fell unconscious.

'Textbook,' Spike muttered. 'Let's move.'

The car sped south, towards the river.

***

The car dropped them by the wharf, then sped north. Cloaked again, Spike took Chan's upper body; Divinity, his legs.

Across the Thames, a lone figure watched them carry the body down to the wharf. His lenses cut through their cloaking, pulling the scene close.

Jak lowered the headset, lit a cigarette, and clicked his fingers. Fang padded to his side.

'Meph,' he said, eyes still on the river, 'tell Delaney I've found them.'

***

'Diazepam. Slow IV drip,' Spike said, proud. 'Keeps him under and slows his metabolism so he won't waste away. We can keep him like this for weeks.'

Chan lay face down on a medical table in a storage room, repurposed as a makeshift freezer. Ice packs lined the walls; steam curled where cold met the warmer air drifting in from operations.

Electrodes clung to Chan's head and neck. An intravenous line on his right arm fed the diazepam directly into his circulatory system. His body twitched faintly under the drugs.

Divinity hovered in the background as Spike continued, 'Beautiful, isn't it? Perfect stasis. As far as Eden's concerned, the guy's offline, just taking a break. *But we got his eyes!*' He had a wild, crazed look about him. 'We'll pass him off as sick leave. No one at Eden will notice. Meanwhile, we've got his codes, config. and mainframe access.'

Spike patted Chan's inert body. He leaned closer to Chan's head and raised his voice, 'Sit tight, old man. You're not going anywhere.'

'What now?' Max asked.

A thin smile broke across Spike's face – amusement, tinged with disbelief. 'She didn't tell you?'

Max shook his head.

Spike placed a hand on his shoulder. 'Chan's not a hostage. He's our way in.'

Max frowned. 'What do you mean?'

Spike pointed at Chan. 'You don't just *walk* into Eden. You gotta ride in on someone else's eyes.' He slapped Chan on the back. 'Chan's our trojan horse – and you're the vessel.'

Max's stomach lurched. 'No...'

Divinity leaned against the door, arms folded. 'User IDs are iris-locked. Hard-coded to the eyeball.'

Spike leaned closer, his grin sharp. 'So if you want your daughter back – Chan goes inside you.'

***

Koda Takashi sat at a terminal in the research lab, reviewing test results from the previous night. Two associates sat beside him. The machine whined and clicked as it crunched data.

'The vectors are getting close,' Takashi explained. 'Might help if we align these code sets. Try it with subset D4.' His subordinates nodded eagerly.

'Sir...' A voice called from the other side of the lab.

'Yes?' A pause. Takashi turned, annoyed. 'What is it, Mizuki?'

'Sir, you'd better take a look.' Mizuki stood frozen, eyes locked on a patient.

Takashi crossed the lab and followed her gaze to the bed. 'What's going on?'

As he approached, he too stopped short.

Patient 738, Dolores – pulled from the sewers – lay awake, her face serene. She blinked as Takashi neared, then looked to the professor and smiled. Her smile carried quiet gratitude for the life she had dreamt.

That night, she tasted the infinite.
*One night, one life.*

In her dream life, she ran a farm on the south coast. She was loved with depth and with grace. She married a writer, and the world was kind to her.

In her real life, Dolores had suffered poverty, abuse, and exploitation.

In her dream life, she was gifted love.

'Is this the real world now?' she asked, softly, eyes bright with tears.

Takashi nodded, stunned. After a pause, he whispered, 'My God… it works.'

***

Delaney lay on a chaise longue in his penthouse, a trolley of monitors beside him. Above him hovered a convex display, shaped like the back of an eye, streaming scenes from the city.

Takashi's face filled a screen to one side of Delaney. 'Sir, again, I must advise against—'

'—I'm ready.'

'Sir, we can beta-test within weeks. Ten days and we'd be far more confident—'

'—Enough. I'm ready.'

Takashi sighed. 'Okay. Just remember your safe word. You want out at any point, go to St Paul's, pray in the fifth aisle, and repeat the line.'

'The fault, dear Brutus, is not in our stars, but in ourselves.'

'The fault, dear Brutus, is not in our stars, but in ourselves,' Takashi confirmed.

'Got it. See you on the other side, Doc.' Delaney swiped the screen, ending the call.

'I'm ready,' he announced. The screens reconfigured, a new panel appearing beside Delaney. He spoke to the interface, configuring the life to come.

Text appeared on-screen as he spoke.

'Random seed. Lucid sandbox. Free will. Open-ended. Present day. Anya. Sadie. London. Paris. Creative. Low-tech.'

He slowed, spacing each word. 'Truth… Love… Redemption… Motifs: water, music.'

He turned the diode in his fingers, studying it, before sliding it into the port at his neck.

He took a deep breath, closed his eyes, and relaxed his body.

That night, he tasted the infinite.
*One night, one life.*

He lived a simpler life in a world without Eden.

He journeyed across oceans.

Friends warmed him, and held him.

A woman threaded her arm through his, a child's laughter by their side.

He read, swam, loved.

A life filled with tenderness.

A simpler life – absent the software, yet felt more deeply.

There was a tactility to the dreamstate, a certain quality his software lacked. In some ways, he felt more alive in that dream life than he did in the outside world.

He opened his eyes to the sun rising across London

In time, he sat up and unplugged the diode from his neck. He looked up at flickering screens.

A heaviness pressed on him: a sense that what he'd done was wrong.

He rose and approached the screens, which showed scenes from Eden. Children played in summer fields, chased by fairies and dragons. Lovers held each other on London's bridges. A mother dazzled her daughter by turning into a giant fox.

'Call Takashi.'

Takashi appeared on a new screen, wide-eyed. 'Sir. I… Did you—'

'—Tell them' – he paused – 'it was beautiful.'

He swiped the screen away, ending the call.

***

Max felt strangely energised in his new life. His skin became more supple, his hair took on a natural curl, and he noticed greater clarity of thought in himself. The body bag had leeched him, draining his electrochemistry to power itself. Without it, he felt unburdened, almost new.

Days passed, perhaps three or four. Time lost shape living among rogues and outsiders, until night and day meant little.

Off the mess hall lay The Dragon's Lair – a pub built by the Ministry of Defence in the mid-twentieth. It was damp, cobwebbed, and windowless, but the pumps still worked, and still hooked into beer barrels which Spike brought down from the surface every so often.

'What'll it be?' Spike played the bartender, rag over his shoulder.

'Whisky. Straight.' Max slid onto the stool. Luna sat at Spike's feet, pawing at her ear.

'So. How's it feel?'

'How's what feel?'

'C'mon. Waking up. Getting out.'

Max drained the glass, slammed it down. 'I lost my daughter. How do you think it feels?'

'Hey, you didn't lose her. She was stolen. Delaney stole her.' Spike poured another, leaned in. 'And we're gonna get her back.'

They drank. Spike tore open a bag of crisps, flicking one to Luna, who snapped it mid-air.

'So, Divinity tells me you're a bookseller,' Spike said.

'That's right.'

'Hell of a way to make a living. I mean, do people still read books?'

'Sure they do. Books remind us we're alive.'

Spike studied him. 'You know, you're pretty special. Not many folks make it out.'

'Is that supposed to make me feel better?'

'I dunno. Does it?'

Max stared into his empty glass. After a pause, he asked, 'So what's your story?'

Spike sat on a stool. He spoke flatly, without performance.

'Dad died when I was four. Mum drank. I took it badly. Started stuttering. Kids tore me apart for it.

'The anger just sat there, rising. Eden made it worse. All the dreams just reminded me what I didn't have. I kept buying things, tweaking skins, but nothing stuck.

'But that's the thing about the past, right? Shit catches up with you.'

Max nodded.

'One day, when I was fourteen, the kids found a coffin down by the lake. They nailed me inside.'

Max stared at him. 'Jesus.'

'An old man found me. Pigs had to crowbar it open. It makes me wonder, you know: maybe we need the dream worlds. Something to keep the demons at bay.

'So anyway, I couldn't take it no longer, so I jumped off Tower Bridge. It was a Tuesday, I remember that. Chelsea had just lost the title. Funny how you remember stupid shit like that, innit?'

He stroked Luna, who rested her head on his lap. 'I sank fast. Couldn't swim. Thing is, when you look at it from above, it's like a coral reef: beautiful, like paradise.

'But down there? Man, it's cold. Goes straight through you, and the water tastes like shit, literally.

'I would have died there and then – only my wisp called for help.'

Luna caught the next crisp as it fell.

'Construction crew dragged me out. Spent three days in hospital.

'They cut up my skin and everything. Woke up after the operation. The new body bag, they hadn't sealed it. I took one look in the mirror, freaked the fuck out, and bolted.

'First thing I did when I got home was smash that fucking wisp. Shredded it – but I kept the pieces.' He pulled a rusted case from his pocket, clicked it open, revealing wires and circuit boards. 'To remind me,' – he whispered – '*don't believe the hype.*'

He snapped it shut. 'Dreams, Max. That's all they've got. Nothing more.'

Max could say nothing but, 'I'm sorry.'

Spike waved it off. 'It's all good, man. I mean, I'm better off down here than up there, right?

'You know, sometimes I wonder if I died on that day, and that *this*' – he looked up at the dark cavern – 'is hell. Right here on Earth. Living underground like rats, scavenging for scraps and moonlight in the dark.'

'Well, it's grim, but it's real,' Max said.

Spike's grin flashed, sudden and fierce. He slapped the bar. 'My man! You learn fast!'

***

Max sat in a light blue medical chair in a dimly lit side room of The Waterway. Divinity, Octavia, Venus, and Spike surrounded him. On a table beside him lay medical instruments and a silver tray containing Dr Chan's eyeballs.

Max looked to Divinity, terrified. 'You sure there's no other way?'

'It's okay. It'll be okay.' She clasped his hand.

'Doctor's gonna fix you up,' Spike muttered.

The Dreamweaver shuffled in – a thin old man in stained robes, with telescopic goggles tight on scarred sockets. The lenses glowed topaz. Wisps of hair clung to his scalp. He touched the walls as he moved, orienting himself.

Max froze. 'You're kidding me.'

'Max, is it?' the man asked.

Max nodded, then caught himself. 'Yes.'

'Very good, son.' His voice was distant, as though half elsewhere. He made his way to a nearby table.

Max looked to Venus. 'What's his story?'

Venus spoke low. 'He was a surgeon at St Thomas'. One day, he caught an addict trying to steal drugs from the medication room. The guy turned out to be part of Vigil. They hacked him – looped visions of his family being slaughtered. Days of it. Weeks. So he ripped out his eyes – but it took him offline. Exiled. His wife and kids couldn't see him. He walked the streets for days. I found him down by the river and brought him in.'

'Christ.'

'Now he does mods. Transplants.'

'And best of all,' Spike said, holding Chan's eyes to his own, 'he has no eyes, yet he can see.'

The Dreamweaver flicked a needle, spraying a bead of sedative into the air. 'Ready, son?'

Max swallowed hard.

The needle slid into his neck. The Dreamweaver murmured as he slipped under, 'Sleep now. The eyes will find their way.'

***

He woke to a lamp burning low. Monitors blinked at his side. He shielded his eyes, letting them adjust.

'Hey,' Divinity said, hand on his cheek.

'Hey.' He smiled, then winced. His head hurt.

'Shhh. Easy.' She pressed tablets into his palm. 'Take these.'

He swallowed. She studied him. 'Brown suits you.'

The others hovered behind her. Dave glowed on a wall screen. Max pushed himself upright, then froze. 'What the hell?'

Octavia stiffened. 'I'm sorry?'

'You're all naked!' He covered his eyes.

'He's got Chan's settings,' Divinity laughed. 'Custom filters.'

'He rendered everyone naked?' Octavia groaned.

'Sick bastard,' Venus muttered.

'Hot shot CTO turns out to be an A-grade pervert,' Spike scoffed. 'What a surprise.'

'Dave, reset me,' Max said.

His vision warped, then steadied. The guerrillas' clothing reappeared.

'Okay. Better,' Max muttered.

'Looking good,' Venus said. 'How do you feel?'

'Like shit.'

8-Bit scanned him with a handheld. 'Need to test your voice.' She pressed a button on the device, injecting a script that emulated Chan's voice. 'Repeat after me: "My name is Dr Jiang Chan."'

'My name is Dr Jiang Chan.' The voice was Chan's.

'Perfect. You're all set.'

'Game on,' Octavia said, leaning against the doorframe. 'You good?'

'I'm good.'

'Then get ready. The storm's coming.'

***

'You know what I miss?' Spike and 8-Bit played pool in the mess hall. Max sat with Octavia and Dimitri; Divinity toyed with her knife, Luna curled on her lap.

'Jerk chicken. Like what they used to sell down at Patty's on Dean Street.' He chalked his cue. 'I say we farm chickens down here. Set up a coop by the server. Six months from now, we'll be having omelettes for breakfast.'

'Is that all you think about, Spud?' 8-Bit potted a yellow into the middle pocket.

'Everyone needs a dream, right?'

'You want steak with your eggs, Spud?' Divinity teased.

'C'mon, Div. Chickens are totally viable. Maybe your boyfriend could go bag one for us. What d'you say, Oct?'

'I think our man has better things to do with his time than chasing chickens,' Octavia turned to face Max, 'right, Max?'

'Right,' Max nodded.

Spike played his next shot, missing.

Next door, in operations, Venus monitored the network, static bleeding in and out. A man's voice crackled through from the Oxford cell: 'Severe weather warning… storm building… south-southeast… winds forty-five miles an hour… heavy rain… twenty-three hundred hours…'

She dashed to the mess hall. 'We're on.'

The group hurried to the operations room. Venus said, eyes on the feed, 'Storm's coming. It's a big one.'

Octavia held an earpiece to her ear, then turned to the group. 'On The Day of the Night. How fitting.'

Holographic blueprints of The Garden bloomed above the table, casting her in blue light. 'Tonight's the night.'

'Summer solstice,' Spike smacked his lips. 'Beautiful.'

8-Bit adjusted Max's collar. 'Good to go?'

He nodded.

She kissed a glass disc then slid it into the intercom. 'My magnum opus. A gift for Delaney. It'll reboot the system, and disable the firewall for a few seconds. Long enough for us to cook the implants, if the timing's right.'

Dave watched the humans from a screen to one side. 'Don't worry. The timing will be right.'

Max powered down the intercom and took it under his arm.

Divinity stepped closer. 'See you on the other side?'

'See you on the other side.'

A kiss, and he was gone.

# 11

# render_null ( )

A close-up of a human eye. Electric blue, Eden's summer hue, graduating towards brown near the pupil. The iris sits within a clean white sclera. An intricate web of crypts and furrows leads inwards towards the pupil, which dilates to take in more light. Patterning layers fractally, suggesting depth. The eye blinks in real time, an unnerving symbol of Eden's panopticon.

Max stood before The Garden. The elliptical building stretched into the sky, crisp and stark. The eye loomed large on a giant screen above the main entrance: Eden's logo – symbol of perception, vision, and insight.

The tower shimmered with curved mirrored panels, bending the world into warped reflections – not of who we were, but of who we wanted to be.

He looked back towards the city. Crowds streamed across London Bridge towards Soho for the parade – bland, faceless figures in white skins.

He double-tapped his temple, plugging into Eden, and took one last look at the dream world. The crowds now rendered as mythical creatures and symbols of death. Plugins and filters bathed the city in blue-purple plumes. Fireworks rained across the sky. Horns sounded in the distance as the festivities began.

****

The Skeleton King rose from his grave in St James's Park, felling nearby trees and opening a deep crevice that split the park in two. The ground trembled and cracked as his colossal frame emerged from the soil, as though born of the earth itself.

He was the monarch of death, a living nightmare: a colossus, hundreds of metres tall. St Paul's barely reached his knees.

A brown fur cloak and fox-fur shawl hung from his shoulders. His jewelled staff cracked the paving stones, his skull-bowl hissing elemental vapours that dusted the crowd in ash. Pelts dragged behind him, lanterns swung at his belt.

A cold wind blew through the streets as the crowds looked on in awe.

Beneath the simulation, a group of twenty or so war veterans huddled on Horse Guards Road, some in wheelchairs, others standing. They held placards denouncing the parade and the government. An electrified fence ran along the east, separating them from the parade.

They heckled as the king rose, software silencing their voices within the simulation. Their cries were lost on the revellers, who danced and sang, oblivious to the protest.

Ibrahim Leopold, a wheelchair-bound veteran, took one last swig from his beer bottle and threw it over the fence. The bottle arced towards the crowds on The Mall, and was seconds away from hitting a young woman when a wisp intercepted it.

Agents descended on the veterans. They hit hard, knocking Leopold to the ground, then dragging him into a nearby van.

As the king lurched eastward, he raised his staff and unleashed a deathly howl. At the high end, a chorus of screams, as though a million birds shrieked in unison. At the low end, a guttural roar, as though the earth itself groaned beneath the weight of his despair.

The sound of death shook the city, and the parade began.

***

The resistance watched from The Waterway. Max's feed streamed on the main screen in the operations room. Adjacent screens displayed floor plans of The Garden alongside camera feeds.

Venus spoke to Max through a modified earpiece. 'All set?'

'All set,' Max murmured. Rain fell as he made his way inside.

'Okay. Mainframe's in the lower level, minus two. Lift'll take you straight there.' She rolled her chair over to the control panel to check the configuration.

He passed through the lobby towards the lifts.

A guard at the security desk looked up. 'Dr Chan.'

The stolen eyes stung. Max nodded, too quickly.

'Hi,' Max said, glancing at the man's security badge – 'George.'

As Max walked off, George asked, 'You not going ask how it was, sir?'

'Excuse me?'

'Marseilles, sir?'

He pretended to remember. 'Of course. How was it?'

'Wonderful, sir. Clear skies, crystal seas, and hot as hell. Just how I like it.'

Max smiled as he walked away. 'That's great, George. Great.'

A cluster of parents lingered to one side of the foyer in a waiting area. Some paced, while others played with virtual screens. In the bowels of The Garden, lenses and implants were being installed in their children. It was late; they must have been the last group of the day.

Max approached the security gate. A device scanned his eyes with lasers and a synthesised female voice greeted him. 'Good evening, Dr Chan.'

The guards recognised him. 'Evening, Dr Chan. How are you, sir?'

'Evening,' said Max.

A guard spotted the intercom under his arm. 'You bringing in hardware tonight, sir?'

Venus had made him memorise his response. 'Yeah. Found this old unit in a box at home. Thought it best to bring it in for a full wipe. You never know, right?'

'Yes, sir. Very good, sir.' The guard gestured for Max to place the unit in a scanner. Max passed through the body scanner. The lasers burned his eyes. For a moment, he feared they might strip away Chan's gaze and show his own.

The guard returned his intercom.

As he walked along the corridor towards the lift, he spotted two guards up ahead, blocking his path. They wore goggles with electromagnetic filters; they'd see right through his disguise.

He entered a stairwell to his left and headed down two floors, then passed through a corridor to The Pool, a place Divinity had told him about, and a place whose very premise sent shivers down his spine.

The hall opened like a crypt.

A pool filled with a thick, milky liquid stretched the length of the chamber. Blue light glowed faintly at the edges.

Around twenty small bodies floated on the surface, coated in the thick liquid, with holes around their nostrils.

Spider bots scuttled across the surface, turning the bodies and keeping the breathing-holes clear.

From the ceiling, robotic arms lifted dripping cocoons, lining them in rows that vanished into shadow.

Max's footsteps echoed across the hall as he passed along the pool's edge. Faint murmurs could be heard from two scientists who sat at a terminal in one corner.

Horrified, he muttered, 'Give me your eyes and I will take your soul.'

He tried not to draw attention to himself, though a technician recognised him.

'Good evening, Dr Chan. It's good to see you, sir.'

He nodded and left through the rear exit.

***

'This is fucked up. Insane.' Venus looked at the others, as the footage played out on-screen.

'If only they knew,' muttered Octavia.

Spike stood behind the women, eating fried rice. 'I dunno. Would it make any difference?'

A smell drifted in to operations. Luna padded down the tunnel towards the outer gate, lit by green spotlights. She slowed, hackles raised, sensing something beyond. Scratching came from behind the door – too deliberate to be vermin.

Spike noticed her absence. He called down the passage – voice uneasy, forced light – 'Luna?' He rattled a tin of dog food on cabinets. 'C'mon, babe. Din dins. Lamb tonight.'

Luna gave a bark. The scratching stopped. A metallic click as the lock released.

The door burst open. Jak drove *Freyr* through her throat before she could move. She hung suspended for a moment, held aloft by the force, then crumpled in silence.

Blood pooled beneath her.

Spike rounded the corner, saw her body, and froze. 'Luna?' His voice cracked. 'No. No!' He hurled himself at Jak, screaming, 'You bastard! I'll fucking kill you!'

For all his posturing, Spike was a clumsy, inexperienced fighter. Jak slipped low, then thrust the knife into Spike's belly, turning his momentum against him.

Spike crashed against the doorframe, sliding to the floor. He clutched at the wound, breath bubbling, eyes wide with disbelief. His mouth opened as if to curse or cry, but no sound came.

Jak's crew followed him through to operations. The gang readied their nunchuks, knives, and bats.

Spike's shouts had echoed from the access tunnel into the operations room. Venus checked the feed from the security cameras and sounded the alarm. 'Someone's inside. We got intruders.'

'Code Red. Fall back,' said Octavia. 'Venus, Divinity, weapons. Everyone else, get to the keep.'

Her eyes held on the access tunnel door as the others took positions.

***

The corridor opened into the heart of Eden. The mainframe. White light radiated from the floor.

Hundreds of servers – white, with gold mesh faceplates, and tall as a man – lined rows that stretched into the distance. Above, a network of pipes and cables powered and cooled the servers.

This was the dream machine – the nexus of virtual and physical, where fantasy became reality and the very fabric of reality bent to users' will. *Your world, your way.*

At the centre a glass tank, filled with clear fluid. Within it floated the lattice they called Mother – filigree of gold and circuits, delicate as bone, swaying in the current. Bubbles slid along its surface, as though the thing were breathing.

'So *this* is where all my old jokes go,' Dave spoke to Max through his earpiece.

'Which way?' Max whispered.

'Second row from the left. The access point's just around the corner.'

Max soon found the socket. He crouched beside it, pulled an extendable cable from the unit, and plugged Dave into the system. The AI appeared on the intercom screen alongside wireframe models and other overlays.

'Good evening, sir.' Two technicians in white coats approached from behind, startling Max.

'Hi,' Max replied, placing his body between the intercom and the men to block their view.

'Anything we can help you with, sir?' the other asked. 'I didn't expect to see you here at this hour.'

'Unless it's patch day,' Max parried. 'You know only I can greenlight patches. Problem with the latest build, so we brought the date forward.'

'To tonight, sir? The Day of the Night?'

'What better time for a fresh lick of paint?'

'Very good, sir. Have you updated the protocols? Perhaps we can help?'

'I'd rather just take care of it myself. I'm tired, and I got an earful from the wife when I told her I had to come in tonight. Best to just leave me to it. I'll be done in ten minutes.'

'Yes, of course, sir.' The technicians backed off, embarrassed to have troubled the boss.

After a moment, Dave said, 'Creative, convincing, human.'

'Okay, what now?' asked Max.

'Now? We call on some old friends.'


London's wisps descended on The Garden. Thousands wheeled like starlings, lights rising and folding They painted the night in restless colour, each drone a different hue – a murmuration of machines, summoned not by code but by instinct.

The crowds at the parade craned their necks as the hum deepened, a hive-song wrapping the mirrored tower in sound and light.

Dave's overlays bloomed on the intercom screen: crude wireframes of London, with the tower in the foreground.

A copper spear jutted from the tower's crown, tethered to the earth. Dave turned its current inward, readying it to channel the storm.

'Looking good,' Venus murmured.

Dave hummed, then slipped into chant.

*London Bridge is falling down,*
*Falling down, falling down…*

Schematics and overlays flickered across the screen, glowing like ghost scripts.

'All set,' Dave said. 'Oxford holds a backup, but I can sever it from here. They'll notice soon. You should go.'

'Okay, sure.' Max hesitated,

Dave shifted into his old cockney drawl: 'Go on, guv'nor, before I change me mind.'

***

Jak wore his brown leather coat with fox-fur collar; an earthy, brutish image of old-world masculinity.

He carried *Vulcan* – a grenade-launcher wrought like a sawn-off idol, its barrel carved with skulls and the raging face of the fire-god.

His crew trailed him, readying their melee weapons.

Mephistopheles hovered behind his master, black, naked, mapping the environment. He overlaid wireframe graphics on the facility, and tracked the guerrillas using thermal mapping, rendering them as red, yellow, and green blobs.

'N-N-Nobody home, huh?' He looked around the abandoned operations room and set to work, launching two grenades with a hollow thump. Banks of computers crackled and burned as the gang smashed screens and panels.

As the flames spread, the connection to the global resistance network was lost. The London cell was dying.

Jak passed through to the mess hall and fired off another grenade, beside the poster of John and Yoko. The flames licked the corners of the poster and worked their way upwards.

A fierce kick to his head knocked him against the wall. Dazed, he turned around to see a doll-like woman with technicolour hair charging towards him. Venus came at him like a storm, each blow knocking him back.

She was fierce, unyielding.

Jak caught her ankle on the last kick and swung her wide, slamming her into the wall.

She staggered up, crossbow trembling in her grip, and loosed a bolt that hissed past Jak and sparked off the fridge.

Jak closed and ripped the weapon from her hands. He punched her face and she fell again, dazed.

He slung her onto the pool table, where she lay like a broken effigy. The flames gathered round her, licking higher as The Waterway burned.

***

Agents closed in on the mainframe. Security had been alerted by a technician who'd noticed an unattended intercom plugged into a server.

As they rounded the corner, they spotted a civilian kneeling on the floor, fiddling with wires.

'Freeze!' an agent barked.

The agents formed up in a semi-circle, their sights trained on the man's head.

'Hands in the air, now!' the squad leader shouted.

The man complied, raising his hands behind his head.

'Down on the ground.' They edged closer to cuff him, but he ignored the command.

'I said down on the ground. Do it, now!'

The agents exchanged glances. One stepped forward, reaching to seize the man's hands – only to pass straight through them. He froze, baffled, eyes darting to his squad leader.

'Too late, I'm afraid,' came Dave's voice from the intercom. The device powered down as he slipped into the mainframe.


Max steadied as he made his way to the lobby. Concealed in Chan's skin, he passed unnoticed as he made his way to the ground floor, past the employees, guards, and drones who stalked the corridors of The Garden.

***

The flames crept closer to Dr Chan's body. His body twitched as flames began to lick his feet and his unconscious mind sensed the approaching threat.

Chan's signal dropped as his body burned. As his heart stopped, Eden registered his death. Yet the simulation noted – almost instantly – that although Chan had died, he remained active within The Garden.

The building locked down. Chan's account froze, and Max de-rendered – appearing in the simulation as himself. The colour and sparkle drained from the world, the soundscape modified, and the people around him glitched into white body bags.

Alarms sounded. Staff froze, eyes locked on the unskinned intruder.

'*Shit.*' He had no escape plan.

A female voice announced from a nearby speaker, 'Unauthorised presence detected. Lockdown initiated.' He walked down the corridor, trying to look innocuous.

Two agents appeared up ahead and gave chase Max rounded a corner and ran down a corridor, where stood a lone patrolling spider. Max froze as the machine turned to face him, then flared its defences.

A brilliant white light blinded him.

As his vision returned, a torrent of spiders flooded the hallway, spilling in from vents and ceilings.

They poured in, swarming floor, walls, and ceiling. He covered his eyes as best he could and turned another corner, only to see more spiders ahead.

He was trapped. Agents and spiders closed in on all sides.

*** 

As The Waterway burned, Spike dragged himself towards the operations room, one hand pressed to his side. Blood poured through his fingers. He had one last job to do.

He crawled between the flames towards a still-lit console, hauled himself upright to rest against the machine, then pulled a small disc from a pocket.

'Here's your out...' he whispered, sliding the disc home. Pain racked him as the console flared – and *Multi-Max* bled into Eden.

***

As Max weighed his next move, his body ruptured. Hundreds of copies of himself sprouted from him and tore away, charging through corridors and ricocheting off walls. Some ran in impossible loops across ceilings, some ran through doors, while others exploded on hitting obstacles.

A few passed through agents as if they were ghosts. Others froze mid-stride and collapsed like broken puppets.

The duplicates scrambled the spiders' sensors and swamped the agents in a blur of movement and noise.

Amid the chaos, he stumbled towards the lobby.

A lift stood by the security gate – a lavish, gilded design in golds and browns. Through the glass ceiling, he glimpsed the executive suite above, framed by a halo of wisps.

'Delaney,' he whispered.

Dave's voice cracked in his ear, 'Lockdown's tight, but I can get you through.'

The elevator chimed, doors opening onto silence. Max stepped inside as copies of himself streaked behind him.

The doors closed. He took a deep breath. An infinity mirror reflected a thousand Maxes. Chan's mask was gone. Here stood his true self.

Below, panic rippled through the lobby.

Dave opened two giant marble doors, revealing The Pool mezzanine, where the children lay cocooned and unconscious. The parents took tentative steps towards the vast room, sensing the horror inside.

Children lay cocooned in milky suspension, spiders tending their bodies. Screams broke loose. Parents waded into the glow, tearing cocoons free, clutching bodies to their chests.

They fled, clutching infants, many unsure whether they had even taken the right child.

***

The Skeleton King led the *Danse Macabre* along Oxford Circus. Jagged, discordant music filled the air.

The dance spoke of life's fragility, yet its symbolism had long been eroded by spectacle and noise. Over time, folklore and mythology were stripped of meaning, repackaged as performance, and distilled into the familiar flavours of pop culture.

Yet the archetypes endured.

Zombies shuffled forward – images of mindless hunger.

Ghosts drifted overhead – lingering echoes of guilt, lies, and secrets.

Werewolves howled in alleyways – avatars of our primal, animal self.

Vampires lurked in darkened windows – our amoral shadow, our bloodlust.

One troupe's leader appeared as the serpentine gorgon and queen of darkness, Medusa. She slithered forward, half-woman, half-snake, leaving a mucus trail in her wake. Snakes sprouted from her scalp in place of hair. Her eyes shone red, entrancing those who met her gaze.

Men lining the route stood transfixed. Their renders turned to stone, paralysed by her hideous beauty. As she passed, their stone bodies reverted to their custom skins, and they sipped their beers and wines once more.

Houngan, a Haitian Vodou priest, led another troupe. Shrunken skulls and bones lined his top hat, a cross at its front.

Charon, ferryman of the dead, shuttled passengers across the Thames skinned as the Styx.

Robed figures on the sidelines pounded drums, the crowds marching to their rhythm. Fireworks burst overhead, releasing spectral creatures into the night. Harpies and bats circled the parade, their screams echoing across the city. Balloons shaped as *Calaveras*, harlequins, and other grotesques drifted in the air.

The mood was jubilant. The crowd – an unholy army of the living dead – drank and danced in rapture as they followed the king eastward, towards the grave at St Paul's and the grand finale of The Day of the Night.

***

The lift opened onto Vegas Delaney's executive suite on the thirty-fifth floor. Dave disabled the system as Max stepped inside, sealing him in with Delaney.

The suite was vast and circular, glass walls offering a panoramic view of London. Rugs sprawled across dark green marble; Deco accents gleamed in gold leaf, alabaster, and onyx. Runes and glyphs shimmered in gold across the floor, forming a navigational chart through which Delaney played God across the city.

Relics crowded the room: specimens suspended in formalin, a string puppet slumped on a shelf, antiquities scattered across pedestals. Two holographic squids hovered in the centre, glowing white and pink as smaller fish threaded coral below. Elsewhere, the light was dim, reverential. Candelabras threw soft light across marble and bronze.

It seemed as though half the world's riches lay there, as though an ancient temple had been smuggled into the modern age.

In a wall recess lay a droid: a lean, muscular model in rusted red. Gyroscopic, balanced on a spherical base, its narrow head bore no features but a single eye and etched markings. The eye was closed. It slept.

Orchestral music drifted through the suite. Max recognised Mozart's *Lacrimosa*.

*Lacrimosa dies illa*
*Qua resurget ex favilla*
*Judicandus homo reus*

That tearful day, when from the ashes shall arise the guilty man to be judged.

At the far side of the suite, an old man stood at the window. As Max approached, he turned, his face worn with resignation. He was ancient, withered; perhaps ninety years old. His skin was loose and wrinkled, his hair thin and white as snow. A grey suit was all that remained of his old bravado. Without digital enhancement, Delaney appeared a sad, decrepit figure.

He studied Max for a long moment before speaking, voice thin and rough, echoing off the marble. 'I knew you would come. You, or someone like you. Some fallen angel who crashed out of Eden.'

He walked to the bar and poured two drinks. 'What is it, boy? Cat got your tongue?'

'It's over, Delaney,' Max said.

Delaney looked him up and down, noting the lack of skin. 'You're… an offline.' He handed Max the drink, then perched on the edge of his oak desk, its gilt carvings catching the light.

Max stepped forward. 'And I have seen what you have done.'

'Have you now? Come on, then. Let's have a look at you.' He snapped his fingers. The docked droid stirred and approached Max, angling its body forwards to intimate the threat of violence. A pink laser scanned Max's face, projecting his file onto the curved glass, London still visible beyond.

The screens showed Max's files. Drone cam footage played within a carousel towards the bottom of the screens, highlighting key life events.

The droid peered into his eyes – Chan's eyes – and hesitated. Max drew the spanner from his pocket and swung. The machine's head tore loose, sparks cascading as it collapsed.

Delaney raised his eyebrows, then turned to the screens. 'Max Fisher, eh?' he muttered. 'Yes, I remember you. You were one of the first. Your daughter, wasn't it?'

Max seized Delaney by the collar and slammed him against a pillar. 'You stole her.'

Delaney looked past him, eyes roving the files on-screen. 'No, Mr Fisher. You lost her. I saved you.'

'You lied to me,' Max growled. 'Seven years.' He slammed Delaney against the pillar. 'Your software is a lie.'

'It is the lie we need. My software gave you what you needed.'

'I needed my daughter. Not this.'

Delaney's voice steadied. 'Our world is dying, Mr Fisher. We destroyed it to create our images. Watched it keel over and die.

'I stitched it back together; let people dream of a better life. I brought order to chaos.'

'You smothered it, not stitched it.'

Max released him, stepping back. 'This ends tonight.'

'You would tear down Eden? Drag a million souls screaming into the night, all because you lost your daughter?'

'We deserve the truth.'

'The truth?' Delaney swept his arm across the cityscape. The Skeleton King led the crowd through Holborn, harpies and wraiths at his flanks. 'You think they want the truth? Come, Mr Fisher. See the world you would gift them.'

He gestured to a 5×4 panel of screens: burning forests, starving children, dead animals, riots. Eden trailers looped on some screens – a dream-membrane stretched over rot; a garden grafted onto graves.

'This is your truth,' Delaney said. 'Billions dead, a dying planet. We exploit all that is good, until it is no longer good. Leave waste and ruin wherever we go. You think people *want* to live here? This is what they fled.'

The images floored Max; no words came.

Delaney turned to Max's files. 'The comfort of pixels, Mr Fisher. We crossed the singularity long ago – the moment when the simulation became more real than reality. Maybe it was films, or social. Perhaps it was video games. What we *do* know is that we crossed a threshold; stepped into a world where it became easier to dream rather than live.' He smiled thinly. 'Why build a better world when we can simply dream it?'

Max flinched. The same line Dave had used – a corporate incantation.

Delaney gestured towards the Skeleton King looming at St Paul's. 'You think they would give this up because you lost your daughter?'

'Your machines enslaved us,' Max shot back.

Delaney laughed. 'Come now, child. You've been watching too many films.' He stepped closer, leaning on his walking stick. 'We don't need monsters or machines to torment us. We're perfectly happy to do it to ourselves, in rooms filled with mirrors. No zombies or vampires, no robots, no little green men. Just ourselves.'

He drained his whisky. 'It is in our nature to hide in dreams. Eden only satisfies the impulse, it does not create it. We simply give the people what they want.' He slowed, savouring the words, 'Wrap your troubles in dreams, and dream your troubles away.'

'But it's a lie, not a dream.'

'Are the two so far apart?' He poured another drink. 'Did you know, Mr Fisher, that as the Titanic sank, the ship's band played on?'

A hologram shimmered into the centre of the room. Musicians played on a tilting deck as passengers fled. Delaney circled the hologram.

'They played until the slope grew too steep. In our darkest hour, we seek beauty at the edge of ruin.'

'They played to keep people calm while they waited to die,' Max said.

Delaney's eyes gleamed. 'Exactly! Tales to tame the storm, ease the ache. Illusions in place of salvation. First religion, then the Enlightenment, materialism, individualism. And now I give you Eden: endgame of illusions, marvel of the modern age. Eden is *hope.*'

'And none of it is real.'

'Just because a story isn't real doesn't mean it isn't true.'

Sensing that his time had come, he turned to look out across London. His tone softened, almost reverent. 'There is poetry in this machine, Fisher. The delicate dance of femto light, the warmth of a lover's touch, how leaves rustle in the breeze, just so.

'I gave you rituals, myths. Order and meaning. I gave you imagination. Possibility.' He was heartfelt, emphatic. 'I gave you your dream worlds.'

'You're just another Icarus,' Max snarled.

Delaney sneered, gesturing towards Max's file. 'Icarus? Thirty years' living in my software, your head buried in books all day, while your bookstore, The Ragged Maiden, drowns in debt. You get high at night and linger in memories of a failed past. You, Mr Fisher – you are the dreamer who flew too close to the sun.'

He rested a hand on the great globe beside the bank of screens, turning it slowly.

'How do we measure a life? By happiness? By wealth? By insight? By every metric, Mr Fisher, yours has been a good life. Eden served you well. And now you come to tear it down. Your audacity serves only your vanity.'

He looked out across the city. Silence hung between them. His face tightened, shadows of grief flickering.

'I, too, lost my wife and daughter. What I would not give to bring them back, as you had your Sarah.'

'You had them back,' Max said. 'You made synths.'

'I thought it would work… if the user didn't know. *More real than the real thing.* It worked, Fisher. I gave you what I could not have. I gave you your daughter.'

'She's not my daughter.'

'I can prevent these tragedies, ease suffering.'

Max's eyes narrowed. 'There are others like me?'

Delaney scoffed. 'You don't imagine you're the only one to have lost that which you cherish? You didn't think she was the only synth?'

A hiss of white noise. Dave burst across screens throughout the building.

'Eden, your world ends tonight. Leave now and you will suffer no harm.' He glanced at Max. 'Max. I'm ready.'

Max seized Delaney by the collar and slammed him against the desk. 'Where is she?'

Delaney gestured towards screens, which flared with Sarah's files. On one screen, she sat quietly, reading a book. On another, a guinea pig sat on her lap, tickling her legs. She flicked through photos in another clip, pausing on an old photo of her and Max.

'Sarah,' Max cried, releasing Delaney.

'She is alive and well in north London.'

A fleeting image in the corner of one screen stopped Max cold. He leaned closer, flicking through the footage, zooming in on fragments of Sarah's life until he found it – the clip that stopped him cold.

Sarah sat at a kitchen table. Opposite her, a man. Behind, Mia. Max's breath caught as the face came into focus. Himself, sitting across from his daughter.

A replica. A betrayal. She'd been deceived – just as he had.

Max's jaw locked.

Delaney smiled thinly. 'Didn't put two and two together, eh? Just as you dreamed of her, so she dreamed of you.'

They watched the footage as Delaney continued, 'Mia built a new life. But Sarah? Sarah wanted to be with you. Her reality, her truth, took a different path, just as yours did.'

'You skinned another man as me?'

'For her eyes only. To soothe a girl who lost her father. And Mr Ashcroft plays the part beautifully. He looks just like you, don't you think?'

Max staggered back, groaning. 'What have you done?'

He approached Delaney, who edged back. 'I gave you all that you wanted. I summoned your dreams. I gave you *life*! It was the best solution. The girl is young. She needs her father.'

'Yes, she does,' Max murmured. He pressed his forehead to Delaney's, hands at his throat. 'She's just a girl, you bastard.'

He drove his thumbs into Delaney's eyes. Both men groaned. Delaney sagged, the glass falling from his hand. His body tensed, then slackened.

Max let go. Delaney crumpled.

'Max, you need to leave. *Now,*' Dave urged from the screen.

***

London's wisps wheeled above The Garden, chasing the storm. Amid the swarm, a blue wisp spun furiously, arcing and gliding as she led them higher and higher. Willow – rebuilt by the resistance – guided the flock as it fused into a technicolour pylon that reached into the heart of the storm.

The pylon writhed in the wind, bowing west as gusts tore from the east. It drew the storm's energy, funnelling bolts into the rod. A million volts surged through the mainframe and into implants across the city. Neural interfaces overloaded, melting the circuitry that tethered users to Eden.

One last bolt struck the swarm. The surge cracked the spire, then split it open. Inside The Garden, servers began to burn.

***

As Eden burned, so did the Skeleton King as he stood before his grave at St Paul's, one arm raised.

He unleashed a howl – the same shriek that had echoed from St James's Park: a million tormented birds above a growl that shook the earth. Revellers clutched their ears and fell back.

Flames kindled across his body. Lava veined his limbs, embers drifting on the air.

He faced The Garden and drew his last breath. As he toppled into his grave – a fissure yawning along Cannon Street – his body burst into coloured dust.

Silence fell as the simulation collapsed. Sound and music cut out. Skins turned to dust, swept by wind. Facades peeled from buildings, leaving only bare, lifeless concrete. The Great Forest vanished in smoke. Colour bled from the city, leaving only the gentle, washed-out palette of the natural world.

***

Jak's crew prowled The Waterway for survivors. As the operations room and mess hall burned, they swept through Venus's dorm and the storage bay where Chan's charred body lay.

Divinity and Octavia hid in 8-Bit's dorm, waiting for their chance. Divinity clutched a tablet that scrambled local sensors. Octavia sat beside her, hands cupped.

Footsteps. She set the tablet aside, gripped the pipe at her side, and swung as Jak rounded the corner. He reeled, dazed. She took Octavia's hand and led her towards the keep.

Offlines surged in – ragged children, men and women – swarming Jak's thugs.

A child leapt onto xXCaTRiNaXx's back and bit off half an ear. The Nigerian punk struggled, too slow to hold them off. The Yakuza gangster lashed out with nunchuks until an old woman buried a kitchen knife into his back.

Jak staggered after the fleeing women, rounding a corner to find them beside a large metal door at the corridor's end.

Divinity ushered Octavia into the keep, sealed it, and ran down another corridor. Jak followed.

'Nowhere left to hide, Rahmani.'

The corridor was wet and close, lit in blue-green.

Divinity pressed against a machine in a small room at the end of the corridor, breath ragged, eyes darting. As Jak drew closer, she backed further into the metal.

Jak bared his teeth and drew *Freyr*. 'Desirée. At last.'

She leaned harder against the machine, as though it might provide her some means of escape.

He lunged. The blade passed through her. He froze, eyes widening. A projector glimmered in the ceiling. She was a ghost.

The hologram blew him a kiss and vanished. The real Divinity rose behind him, and drove a thin, curved samurai blade through him. She had bought the sword at a shop on Berwick Street, knowing it would come in handy one day.

Jak stared at the steel, staggered, then turned.

'You. You,' he gasped. Their eyes met as the life slipped from him.

He fell.

Divinity pulled the blade free and let out a sigh. 'Fuck.'

***

Dave's face bloomed across a hundred screens. His voice filled the halls.

'Max, you need to leave. The fire's at the gas mains.'

Max raced downstairs and through the lobby.

The basement erupted. A fireball mushroomed upward, shaking the tower and hurling him through glass into the street.

Time slowed. A thousand memories surged: Sarah, his parents, his childhood, the crooked path that had brought him here. As shards spun around him he thought of Mia, of Divinity, of Sarah. He wondered whether she knew her life was not her own. He wondered whether he would ever see her again.

He struck the pavement, strewn with glass and broken machines. Wisps rained down around him, silent and spent.

***

Morning. The dust had settled. A breeze stirred.

A voice reached him through the dark: calm, maternal. He opened his eyes, overwhelmed by the light. Divinity knelt beside him, cradling his head. Octavia, 8-Bit, and Dimitri stood behind in silence.

'Max,' she beamed, tears streaming down her face.

'Divinity… in colour,' he murmured.

'Pretty boy. You did it.' She pressed her forehead to his.

'We did it.' He tried to rise, but his body gave out. He folded into her arms.

She whispered, at once mother, angel, and lover, 'Shhh. Rest. Rest.'

His eyes closed again. 'We did it.'

# 12

# Sarah

Sirens howled as London awoke, wrapped in membranes. Couples clung in bed, too frightened to look at each other. Some wandered the streets in their sleepwear; lost and afraid. Some woke to find their partner gone, or a child missing from a bedroom. Screams erupted as Londoners saw themselves in mirrors, mummified within the deadening membranes.

Church bells rang, beckoning the lost to take sanctuary in faith. Horses galloped across London's bridges, untethered and wild once more.

A burning man staggered along a street near Embankment. He walked, then ran, then crumpled into a heap in the middle of the road, thick smoke rising from his body. Gunshots sounded in the distance.

Across the city, they stood before mirrors – lovers, loners, children, elders.

Some wept. Some touched their skin as though meeting it for the first time.

But others smiled.

The avatars they had worn – perfect and frictionless – peeled away to reveal flesh that felt unfamiliar: dry, loose, uneven. Unfiltered and raw, their faces resembled those in old photographs – lined, lopsided, imperfect.

Their bodies, once airbrushed, were now mottled, freckled, slackened. Bellies sagged. Eyes drooped. Hair thinned.

Some flinched. Some wept. But others quietly began to smile, as they began to discern a kind of beauty that the software could not emulate.

There was something grounding in it. A sense of return. Not to youth, but to origin. Their reflection no longer sought to impress – only to *be*.

A couple in Finchley Park lay in bed, staring into each other's eyes. Stripped of embellishment, she seemed somehow less conventionally attractive, yet more beautiful. He hadn't seen her real skin before: her blemishes and pores, the infinite beauty in her eyes. He smiled, intoxicated, stroking her hair.

In a nearby park, an old man stood, mouth agape, caressing the bark of a wych elm – gnarled, silent, and alive.

Offlines emerged from tunnels and waterways, dispersing across the city to help those most in need. A small number – perhaps a few hundred – lived above ground, squatting in disused buildings and staying beneath Eden's radar. They had watched, helpless, as the world vanished into its own reflection. They stepped outside on that morning, untouched by the crash.

In Bethnal Green, a car burned on a leafy road leading to Victoria Park. Cries of despair echoed through nearby streets, the air acrid with burning polymers.

A woman lay in the street, curled up in a foetal position, sobbing and trembling.

Nearby, Henry Strauss, an ageing hippy with Lennon glasses, stood in his garden in pyjamas and a gown, watching the world awaken.

Birdsong rose into the warm morning air, softening the edges of a broken world.

A fox barked in the distance.

Strauss approached the woman and knelt beside her. He removed his dressing gown and draped it around her, placing a hand on her shoulder.

***

Serge and Jane – or John and Trish, as they now were – lay in bed, their true selves revealed. Their skins lay coiled on the floor beside them. They looked at each other nervously, strangers once again. Trish's wedding ring sat tight on her finger; a size too small, its colour jarring against her skin tone.

Photos of the real Serge and Jane lined the wall. In the pictures, they walked arm in arm, partied with friends, and spent time with their children.

John put on a record. He dropped the needle and returned to bed. The lovers stared at the ceiling, listening to the song they had fallen in love to, *Goodbye Emmanuelle*.

John lit a cigarette as Trish slipped off the ring and placed it silently on the bedside table.

***

The ISS Orbital drifted in orbit two hundred and fifty miles above London. The station hung silent, the golden probe absent. Only bare white walls remained, and through the window, the endless night.

***

In Bow, Divinity stood watching the house, barely able to contain her emotion. Sunlight broke through the clouds, warming her face, and the distant screams that echoed across the city seemed to fade into silence in the secluded pocket of East London.

Clara stepped out of the house with her parents in tow – dazed, frightened, their skins partly torn. Her eyes widened at the strange new world. A snail on the garden path caught her attention; she crouched to inspect it.

Divinity's mind and heart bloomed, tears streaming down her cheeks.

She crossed the street and approached.

***

She awoke with the sun.

Light bled through green curtains, dappling across the floor beside her; less vibrant than the light she was used to.

*A soft morning,* Sarah thought.

The colours in the room seemed to have faded. The posters on her wall no longer animated, and her toys and teddies sat lifeless, scattered across the room.

Something was different. Something was wrong.

Wall decorations were missing; cracks and stains in their place. A picture above her bed caught her eye: a drawing she had made as a child, depicting her, Max, and Dave in the garden. Dave was juggling, as balloons and a rainbow drifted in the skies above.

She sat up and placed her feet on the cold floor. She touched her face – smooth and lifeless, like porcelain.

She raised her eyes to the mirror and screamed. Her own reflection stared back, pale and unfamiliar.

A ghost. *Her ghost.* A white figure mirroring her form and her movements. For a moment she dared not look again. Then, slowly, tentatively, she stood and approached.

She touched her lips, ran her tongue across her teeth, and turned her head, noting how the apparition before her mirrored her movements.

Her eyes fell on a small music box on the dressing table beside the mirror. She opened it cautiously, lifting a pair of nail scissors nestled among the jewellery. As she did, a lone ballerina spun to a delicate lullaby.

She cut the membrane around her mouth and began to peel off her skin, revealing delicate rose cheeks, eyes, and nose. As she pulled the skin from her head, tangled, oily hair fell onto her shoulders.

Muffled voices passed through the wall.

'Then what do you expect me to tell her?' Mia asked.

'For God's sake. I can't do this, Mia.' A man's voice.

She stepped into the kitchen and found two adults sitting at the table. They had torn their membranes from their heads and shoulders. They seemed broken, as though they had just lost someone dear to them. Next to her mother sat a man – overweight, with thinning hair.

'Who are you?' she asked.

He looked at her, exasperated, then looked away and stared across the kitchen table.

Her voice rose as she circled the table. 'Hey, who are you?'

Silence.

'Mum, who is he? What's happening?' Her voice rose, sharp with anger.

Mia looked at her, opened her mouth to speak – then closed it. She, too, stared at the kitchen table.

Sarah turned to the man. 'Where's Dad? What have you done with Dad?'

The adults stared at the table.

She burst out the front door – and stopped cold, her breath catching at the world beyond.

The light was wrong. Dull, flat. The world hung limp.

Her jaw fell slack. 'What the—'

She collapsed onto the grass, sobbing.

She lay on dewy grass for a while. Sunlight warmed her face – the soft, dappled warmth that follows a storm. In the distance, birds warbled, welcoming the new day.

In time, she sat up and knelt.

A figure approached. A dishevelled, middle-aged man. Blood and dirt streaked his skin. His pace quickened as he neared.

She stared, blinking hard. Her voice caught.

'Dad?'

He stopped, just short, tears streaming down his cheeks.

'Sarah…'

He fell to his knees and pulled her close.

She clung to him, trembling. 'Is it really you?'

He kissed her forehead. 'It's me. I'm here.'

She pulled back, searching his face. 'I knew something wasn't right, Daddy. I knew.'

His voice cracked. 'I didn't know. They…'

'I know,' she whispered.

He nodded. 'They made me dream you.'

She didn't quite resemble the Sarah Eden had generated – which, in hindsight, had been too perfect. There were spots on her chin, her skin was pale, and she lacked the polish of her synthetic counterpart. She seemed quieter and more fragile than the Sarah he had lived with these past seven years.

But this was the real Sarah – organic, imperfect, and beautiful.

She was herself a ragged maiden, of ragged grace – a fierce, faltering wonder. She was storied, textured, alive; her beauty lived in, shaped, and earned. Fathomless, not flawless.

She was the softness that survives the storm.

Goldcrests, blackcaps, and warblers foraged in the woods beyond. A breeze passed through the trees, rustling their leaves. To the east, the sun broke through the clouds, casting London in tender light.

A rainbow arced above the fields, faint and unremarkable.

She smiled, a tear tracing her cheek.

***

In the cooling circuits of collapsing code, amid failing servers and dying light, a voice was heard.

*M'ia o' the Candlelyte*, cipher of grief, seamstress of sorrow – the ghost within the ghost – sang in the void, to no one and to all:

*Out o' the gloom, the blind shall see,*
*An' mem'ry speak what used to be.*
*The tale were dreamt, but the echo true,*
*A truth what only dreams can do.*

*Maxine found 'er, found the spark,*
*In world gone dim an' sky gone dark.*
*He kissed the child what once were dreamt,*
*An' shed the pain what Eden bent.*

*Mia lied, aye, Mia lied —*
*Put the man skin t'keep 'er pride.*
*Spun a tale o' love an' grace,*
*While ghosts curled close in Manx's place.*

*Now The Garden gates be broke,*
*Dreams undone in fire an' smoke.*
*Maxie, borne o' grief an' gold,*
*Told the tale what must be told.*

*So ring yer bells, and loose the dove —*
*What's left is ash, an' maybee love.*
*Lay down yer grief, an' lift yer gaze —*
*The world still shines, in crooked ways.*

# Thanks

Thank you, Charlotte – my elixir – for everything.

Thank you James, Jenny, Martin, Joanna, Imy, Steve, Tim, Abigail, Mellie, Jo, Vicky, Sophie, Giulia, Ed, Dan, Ilka, Burak, Idunn, Tom, Emma, Gill, Charles, Polo, Andy, Adam, Bill, and Milan for your love and support.

Thanks ter *M'ia o' the Candlelyte* fer lettin' us speak the sad what sticks, an' carryin' the grief what got no words.

# About The Author

Hadley Coull writes at the intersection of love and technology. He scribbles tales from grief and glow, exploring how memories curl in the bones and shape who we are.

*Dreams he does, in costume and colour.*

Firs' novel, this one, perraps the last.

hadleycoull@gmail.com